BRAIDED SILVER

UNTOLD TALES: RAPUNZEL

LAURA GREENWOOD

© 2020 Laura Greenwood

All rights reserved. This book or parts thereof may not be reproduced in any form, stored in any retrieval system, or transmitted in any form by any means – electronic, mechanical, photocopy, recording or otherwise – without prior written permission of the published, except as provided by United States of America copyright law. For permission requests, write to the publisher at "Attention: Permissions Coordinator," at the email address; lauragreenwood@authorlauragreenwood.co.uk.

Visit Laura Greenwood's website at:

www.authorlauragreenwood.co.uk

Cover Design by Vampari Designs

Braided Silver is a work of fiction. Names, characters, places, and incidents are the products of the author's imagination or are used fictitiously. Any resemblance to actual persons, living or dead, businesses, companies, events, or locales is entirely coincidental.

BLURB

Twenty women. Five tests. One Prince, and a pauper determined to win.

When Cosette is taken away from her tower, and sent to the palace for having silver blood, she ends up competing for a chance to win the Prince's hand in marriage.
With new friends, rivals, and a kitsune familiar, can she win the Prince's heart? Or will she find herself locked back up in her tower?

-

Braided Silver is a fantasy romance retelling of Rapunzel and is part of the Untold Tales series.

CHAPTER ONE

THE STARS WINKED at me from high in the sky, and I searched among them for the one I'd named Fairy Godmother as a child. My gaze locked on her, in the same place she'd been since the first time I'd found her, twinkling in the dark. I knew now that it was nothing more than part of the dark sky, but as a child, I'd been fascinated by the things I'd read in books about Fairy Godmothers, royalty, and magic, and how they'd sweep away young girls who had been trapped or forced to do things against their wills.

The fact I'd been locked in a tower my entire life probably had something to do with the obsession. Though it was a little different when I was able to leave at will. Not that Mother knew. And without any money, or way to make it, there was no point running for good. I always came back, even if there was a small part of me that didn't want to.

I sighed loudly. "I wish you were real." Then she *could* whisk me away to a better life.

The star twinkled in response. Something I used to believe was an answer.

I flashed it a sad smile. There was nothing she could do about my situation. The only person who'd be able to change it, was me, and I didn't have any idea where to begin.

A loud clunk sounded, and I knew that meant Mother was returning. At least she'd finally stopped demanding to use my hair as a weird kind of ladder and I'd finally managed to cut it to a manageable length. Though hanging down to my knees probably wasn't deemed to be sensible by most, but I didn't care. It was still taking a lot of getting used to, which was the one reason I hadn't cut it further. I was still surprised she'd let me do it. Perhaps climbing up hair wasn't the easiest way to get places.

For a few weeks after I'd cut it, I watched Mother to see what she did to get in and out of the tower, which was how I'd learned of my escape route, even if I didn't use it as often as I should.

"Cosette?" she demanded from the room down below. Considering we lived in the tower completely on our own, it was odd we only used three floors of it. All at the top. It was like she *wanted* to make it obvious she was up to no good. I'd always wondered what she'd done to make herself a fugitive.

"Coming," I shouted back, pulling away from the window. If I didn't go see what she wanted, then I'd only end up punished for it later.

I swished my hair over my shoulder and made my way down the stairs, resisting the urge to run. I used to feel like I had to every time she called, but recently, I'd been trying to teach myself to not give in to her too easily. So far, she hasn't said anything about it, so there was some hope I'd be successful. Perhaps now I was an adult myself she'd let me leave the tower and work some kind of job. That would be nice. I wanted to see the world.

"Good evening, Mother," I said as I stepped off the stairs and into the room we used as a living space. It had a tiny stove in the corner, along with a staircase which led to the lowest level we used, which housed a pantry, and a well. I had no idea how the well had ended up in there, it had to have been built into the tower when it was constructed, otherwise, it would make no sense.

"Ah. You're here."

Because there was somewhere else I'd be? I bit my tongue so the words didn't slip out. I was always careful with *when* I snuck out for this exact reason. I had no idea what she'd do if she caught me, but I wasn't in a hurry to find out.

"Yes," I said instead.

"I'm going away for a few days." She walked over to the table we ate at and ran a finger over it. "Perhaps you should give this place a proper clean while I'm gone."

Anger bubbled up inside me. Our tower *was* clean. I took great pride in keeping it that way, and only partly because I had nothing else to do.

"Where are you going?" There was no point in asking. She went away like this at least once a month, but wouldn't tell me where she went. And yet, that never stopped me asking. One day, I'd find out. She couldn't just disappear for a few days at a time and not go anywhere.

"There's enough food in the pantry. But don't eat more than you need to. I'll be able to tell if you have." She studied me sternly, as if I didn't already live my life by the rules she instilled in me as a child.

Keep the tower clean. Don't eat more than you need. Don't ask questions. Don't ask to leave the tower. Don't go into her workroom even to clean.

I could recite them in my sleep, if she needed to. And I'd only ever broken one of them.

Probably the worst one, in her eyes. I imagined she'd frown on it, then find some way to punish me.

Though I wasn't sure what that would be. While she didn't show much affection towards me, she also didn't hurt me. I hoped that meant she loved me on some level, even if I wasn't sure what that was.

"Of course, Mother."

"There's a pile of clothing that needs repairing too," she added. "Make sure that's done."

"I will do," I promised. "When are you leaving?" I hoped she'd say tonight. While it was dark outside, it wasn't too late for me to sneak out if she left straight away.

"I'll leave at dawn," she said.

My heart sank. I guessed that meant I'd have to wait to sneak out. Though dawn would mean she'd be gone for the entire day, and I could make my way into the town. Hopefully, Archie would still be about that early. I normally met him in the early evening. Sometimes, we missed one another, but never by very much.

"Do you need me to pack anything for you?" I asked.

"No. And you're not to disturb me for the rest of the evening. I'm going to be in my workroom." She didn't wait for me to respond and swept passed me, heading up the stairs and into the room she kept locked.

Not for the first time, I wondered what she did in

there, but I suspected it wasn't something I'd ever have the answer to.

With nothing else to do, I headed to the stove and made myself some tea. And then, I could plan what I was going to do in the village tomorrow. At least I had that to look forward to.

CHAPTER TWO

THE PANTRY ROOM was as dark as always, and a little colder than I liked. Not that it mattered, I wouldn't be here long. Mother thought this way out of the tower was a complete secret to me, but she was wrong. I'd seen her use it often enough to have worked it out for myself. If she hadn't wanted me to know about it, then she should have made sure I was unconscious before she left.

I pushed on the secret door and waited for it to swing open. Before stepping through, I slipped my hand into the pocket of my simple dress to make sure I had the key still. The last thing I wanted was to get trapped *outside* the tower with no way of getting back in. Then I'd have to work out how to run away with no money, and no means to make it, or I'd have to wait for Mother and she'd learn my secret.

Neither of those appealed to me. Actually, that wasn't true. Running away appealed, but it wouldn't be easy.

Assured by the heavy weight of it, I left and went through the door and made my way down the stairs. I trailed my hand down the wall to make sure I didn't stumble. There wasn't anything to light my way, which made it slow going.

Once I reached the bottom, I left through a not-so-secret door. I supposed there was no reason to hide this when I couldn't see it. Which did raise a lot of questions. Like why Mother wanted me to stay in a tower and never leave. I'd tried asking her a couple of times, but she always ignored it when.

The walk into the village was only a short one. It had surprised me the first time I'd ventured out of the tower. If I were keeping a secret, I'd want to be further away from people. Then again, I supposed it made sense. Whether or not we were hiding from the world, we needed to eat, and the village was the best place to get food from.

I turned into the square and my heart skipped a beat at the sight of the tall blond man standing by the well.

Despite knowing it wasn't ladylike, I held my

skirts up a little so I could free my legs easier. And then I broke into a run.

It only took a moment for Archie to notice and rush towards me. He caught me in his arms and spun me around, making me giggle.

He set me down on my feet and leaned in, pressing his lips against mine. My eyes fluttered closed and I pressed into him, enjoying the way he made me feel. Everything around us faded away, no longer mattering to me.

We pulled away from one another, both grinning widely.

"I didn't think you'd be here," I said.

"It's a month since you last got out of your tower," he pointed out. "I always come and wait."

"Oh." A blush rose to my cheeks. It was silly to feel this way. I knew Archie liked me. Not only had he told me, but we'd been meeting one another like this for months. Maybe even for a year.

"What do you want to do today?" he asked.

"Whatever you want to." We always had the same exchange. He was the one who had money after all.

I wasn't sure what he did to earn it, but he always had a ready supply and assured me he could afford the things we bought. I didn't ask many questions about it because a small part of me was afraid of the answer. What if he was some kind of outlaw? I'd heard they were responsible for a lot of lost wealth in the area.

"It's still early, so we could collect the things for a picnic then go for a walk?" he suggested.

I nodded eagerly. "That sounds nice. We could go down to the waterfall?" We didn't get many full days together, so it would be nice to take advantage of this one by going to that spot.

"Sounds good to me."

He held out his arm to me and I rested my hand on it. I loved it when he did this. It made me feel as if I was a proper lady and he was walking me around a fancy court while everyone whispered about what a good couple we made. I knew that was ridiculous, and I hadn't told him about the fantasy, but it was there.

After stocking up everything we needed from the local stalls and shops, we made our way to the waterfall. It was several hours' walk away from the village, but I didn't mind. The only consequence for me was that I got to spend more time with Archie, and that wasn't exactly a hassle.

The low rumble of the waterfall grew louder as we approached, and I took in a deep breath, enjoying the fresh scent in the air and the peace it brought. I had no idea why more people didn't come here. Perhaps they thought it was cursed, or something like that. I'd heard a lot of the villagers talk about superstitions like that before.

Archie shrugged off his coat and laid it out on top of one of the rocks for us. I took my seat, spreading my skirts around me so I'd be comfortable. They weren't anything fancy, so it didn't matter if they got dirty.

"Do you want to eat now, or later?" Archie asked as he sat down beside me. The small bag we'd filled with food and drink sat between us.

"Later." I wanted to enjoy the company and the scenery first. There was something so beautiful about this place. "I'm glad you were here today."

He chuckled. "I've been waiting for you every day this week."

"Oh. I'm sorry, I couldn't get away sooner..."

He reached out and took my hand in his, giving it a squeeze. "I know how it is. But you don't have to go back there, Cosette. You could come away with me and live a better life."

My eyes widened. He'd hinted that he'd be interested in that more than once, but he'd never outright offered.

"Where would we go?"

"Back to my lands," he admitted. "My parents have decided that it's time for me to get married."

"Oh. So you want me to come back as your

mistress?" Hurt lanced through my heart, but a small part of me was still convinced I'd take the offer as a chance to be close to him.

"What? No. Of course not," he insisted quickly. "I want to make you my wife."

My jaw dropped. That wasn't an offer I'd expected him to make, no matter how much I'd wanted him to.

"You really want that?" I whispered.

"Of course. Why wouldn't I?" The earnest look he gave me was enough to know how serious he was.

The only problem was Mother. I had no idea why she wanted me to stay in the tower all the time, and a part of me had always assumed I'd find out before I left. But if I left with Archie now, then I'd have a couple of days head start on her finding out, and dragging me back. That could only be an advantage.

"If you're sure..."

"I am," he assured me. "It's a little bit more complicated than just coming home with me, but it won't be a problem."

I frowned. "What does that mean?"

The waterfall called my attention away from him. Mostly because I needed some time to process what he'd said.

"I can't really explain until we get there. But if

you pack your bags and meet me in the square tomorrow, then I promise, I'll explain on the way."

I frowned. Why couldn't he tell me about it now? That made no sense.

"I'll think about it." The words hurt to say, but there was no getting around them. I couldn't run away from my tower and into the unknown, that was the reason I hadn't already done it.

He reached out and squeezed my hand. "Please do. Nothing would make me happier than if you were my wife."

"I hardly know anything about you," I pointed out.

"You know me better than anyone."

I let the words sink in, trying to work out if they were true or not. In some ways, I could see how they were. We'd talked about a lot of things during our meetings, and they'd happened every month, which was a lot of time. But I didn't know what he did for his living, or who his parents were. I didn't even know where he lived.

"I'll think about it," I repeated.

He rubbed a hand over his face. "All right. I'll be waiting tomorrow anyway. Hoping you'll show up."

I nodded. There was nothing more to say on the matter before I'd thought things through.

"Why don't we eat now?" I suggested, hoping it would distract both of us.

"Good idea." He started getting the food out, spreading it out around us.

We ate in silence, enjoying the freshly baked bread with creamy goat's cheese, and sweet honey. I pushed away the guilt that I hadn't paid for any of this. No matter how many times Archie assured me he didn't mind, sometimes, it didn't help.

After eating, it was easy to slip back into our easy patterns of conversation. We knew how to talk to one another, and despite his offer hanging over my head, we did.

CHAPTER THREE

"Will I see you tomorrow?" Archie asked as he looked down at me.

His arms were around me, offering warmth and protection which only he could give.

"I still don't know," I admitted. "Maybe?"

He nodded. "That's not a no. I'll take it. For now."

Relief washed through me. He hadn't pushed me on the subject after we'd eaten, or even while we'd been walking back from the waterfall. But now we were saying goodbye, I could understand why he wanted to bring it up again. He needed it to be something I thought about while I made my way back home. And for the rest of the night.

"I promise, I'll think about it."

"That's good enough."

I could hear the *for now* even though he didn't say it.

He lifted a hand and brushed it against my cheek. My eyes fluttered closed as I leaned into his touch. No one made me feel the way he did. Though that wasn't a big surprise. I'd not spent as much time with anyone else. I'd been coming into the village since before I'd met him, but none of the other men, or women, had made the same impression.

His lips pressed against mine, and I leaned into him, enjoying the moment. I was glad he respected me enough to let me sleep on my decision. If he asked me right now, I'd have caved instantly.

"I have to go," I murmured once we'd broken the kiss. It was getting dark, and I didn't want to be walking alone when too late. That was a good way to get myself killed.

"I know," he whispered against my lips. "But if this is my last moment with you, then I want to make the most of it."

Pain lanced through my heart. Why was I even thinking about this? I should tell him that I wanted nothing more than to spend the rest of my life with him. Delaying that decision wasn't a good idea.

No. It was. Leaving with him would mean I had to leave my entire life behind. And while Mother wasn't exactly the loving and caring type, she was still my only family. That and the tower being the only home I'd ever known was tripping me up a little.

"I can come back tomorrow no matter what my answer is," I suggested.

He nodded. "Please. Then if you say no, I can properly say goodbye." He paused, as if reluctant to say whatever he was thinking next. "My parents won't take no for an answer when it comes to me getting married. They want me to have a bride by the end of the year."

I bit my lip but nodded, grateful he was being honest with me, even if it was hard.

He leaned in and kissed me again. "I'll see you tomorrow?" he checked.

"Yes. I promise."

Our embrace ended and he stepped away from me, leaving a sudden chill to wash over me. I resisted the urge to tell him I'd been wrong and I didn't want him to leave. I wasn't one to make rash decisions.

I waved at him, then turned away and started walking. It was easier if I didn't say goodbye to him. I couldn't bear the word when it could be the last time I said it to him.

The sky darkened quickly and I glanced up as I walked to see if I could see my Fairy Godmother star. I could ask her for guidance, even if I knew she was only a star and wouldn't have any advice to give.

Much to my disappointment, she wasn't out yet. I'd have to wait until later to ask for her help, and hope that in doing so I'd work out what the right answer was for me when it came to Archie. My heart wanted more than anything to say yes to him, but that didn't mean I should.

I looked over my shoulder to see him one more time, but I'd walked further from the village than I'd realised, and he was no longer watching me.

I tried not to be too disappointed by that. If walking away was hard now, what would it feel like to turn my back on him forever? Could I survive that?

The sound of rustling leaves caught my attention and I froze where I was standing, trying to work out what direction it was coming from. I took a deep breath and counted to ten, trying not to get too freaked out by it. Chances were it was a small animal going about their evening foray and had knocked the leaves in the process.

When I was satisfied there was nothing more sinister afoot, I let the noise wash over me and carried on. I needed to get home, especially if I might need to pack a bag before I left in the morning. It was a good job Mother would still be away for a few days, that way I'd have a head start and she wouldn't be able to drag me back to the tower.

Another rustle caught my attention. Instead of stopping again, I quickened my pace. It was probably another animal. It had to be. The alternative didn't warrant thinking about.

Even so, it would be better if I got back to the tower quickly. I checked that the key was still firmly in my pocket again. The last thing I wanted was to get back and find myself locked out.

More sounds came from within the trees. It was starting to worry me now, especially as I was far enough away from the village that no one would hear me if I cried out for help.

A shiver ran down my spine. What was I going to do? I had no way of defending myself, and no one within helping distance. I supposed I could run, but what would that matter?

Especially when this could all be in my head.

Darkness was falling fast now, and it was making it difficult to see. I should have left Archie earlier, but it had been hard to tear myself away, especially with the way he'd been talking.

Now I might be about to pay the price of that.

Something moved in front of me, the hulking shadow blocking my path. I stopped in my tracks, not wanting to walk into whatever was waiting for me.

More sounds came from the left.

Panic began to rise inside me, but I pushed it down. I had to stay calm or I stood no chance of getting out of this situation unharmed.

"Is anyone there?" I called out. "I'm meeting my husband around the corner." The lie probably wouldn't convince anyone, but it was worth a try.

A man chuckled.

Oh no. That wasn't good. I didn't stand a chance against one man, never mind multiple. And from the sounds coming from the bushes, that was what I had to deal with.

With the way in front of me blocked, there was only one direction I could go. I didn't waste any time, and spun on my heels, lifting my skirts higher than was proper. Without hesitating, I set off back in the direction of the village, running faster than I ever had in my life. I didn't bother crying out for help. I was too far away for anyone to hear, and it was better if I saved my breath so I could keep running.

Grunts and shouts sounded behind me as the men started to follow. I'd been right. Somehow I wasn't happy about that.

I stumbled on a tree root, but managed to keep

on my feet. I was lucky to. One more mistake like that and I was going to end up caught. I didn't know what the men wanted with me but all the guesses I had didn't end well for me. I'd rather avoid the consequences of being caught if I could help it.

Someone lurched into the path in front of me and I finally let out a scream. He came at me and I stumbled back, falling to the floor.

I closed my eyes, not wanting to see what was about to happen. I'd fight every step of the way, but I doubted it would do anything to save me.

"Get the hood on," one of the men grunted.

The next thing I knew, rough hands were shoving something over my head. I opened my eyes to find myself surrounded by blackness. I wasn't sure whether to be relieved or terrified that they were blindfolding me.

I kicked out against them, but without being able to see where they were, it was almost impossible to make a difference. One of them grabbed hold of my feet and bound them together. There went any chance of running away. My hands were next. The rough twine bit into my wrists and caused me to cry out. The men didn't respond to the sound. It had probably been muffled by whatever was over my head.

Tears rolled down my cheeks. What was happening? I shouldn't have left Archie. If I'd gone with him, then I wouldn't be in this situation. I could have been safe in his arms and on my way to becoming his wife.

"Get her in the cart. We have an appointment to keep," one of the men barked.

Someone picked me up and threw me over their shoulder with ease. I'd never stood a chance when it came to getting away. These men were always going to be able to bring me where they wanted me to go.

He strode a few feet and dumped me unceremoniously into the base of a wooden wagon. It creaked and moaned, but I couldn't tell any more about it from how I was lying.

I had no idea where they were taking me and knew better than to ask.

The only thing I could focus on was the question of what was going to happen to me.

CHAPTER FOUR

I STRETCHED my limbs as consciousness returned to me. Though if I thought about it, I had no idea when I'd *lost* it. Potentially some time on the cart. I ran my hands over my head, trying to check nothing was bruised or bumped. It was only when I was halfway through I realised my arms and legs were no longer bound.

Satisfied I hadn't been knocked out, I turned my attention to my new surroundings.

Ah. I appeared to be in a small room with harsh stone floors and metal bars across the front of it.

I was in a cell. And had no recollection of how I'd gotten here. I shouldn't be in jail. Not when I hadn't done anything wrong. Unless I counted leaving my tower, which I didn't. No one would think that was bad other than Mother. And potentially me, depending on how this situation played out.

"Ah good, you're awake," someone said from outside the door.

I focused my attention on them. Unlike the men who had captured me, this man was skinny and not much taller than me. He was the kind of person I could get the best of if it came to a fight.

"Where am I?" Perhaps if I knew that, I would be able to make a plan to escape and get back to the village before I was supposed to meet Archie.

Pain lanced through me. What would he think when I didn't show up? I'd promised him I would no matter what I decided. Would he think I was avoiding him? I doubted he'd come to the conclusion that I'd been taken by people I'd never met.

"You're at a testing facility," the man said.

"I don't know what that means." I climbed to my feet, stumbling a little as I did. Had I been put to sleep using some kind of herb or potion? That would explain why I had no recollection of it. But my head had been covered for all the time I remembered.

"The Silver Blood testing centre," he tried again.

I shook my head. "What even is that?"

He sighed, as if I was disappointing him with my ignorance. I sort of understood. I was annoying myself with it too.

"You're here to be tested for Silver Blood."

I frowned. "But why?" I didn't even know what Silver Blood was, how would I know if I had it?

"There are rumours that someone with Silver Blood lives in these parts. The men who brought you in last night were to hired to hand you over for testing and collect their reward."

"Reward?" I echoed. This didn't make any sense.

"Did they not tell you any of this?"

"They were too busy kidnapping me to bother with explanations," I muttered.

"Well, you'll be tested before the day is out."

"And what happens then?" I asked.

He shrugged. "That depends on your results."

"Hands out," someone barked from further down the corridor.

Despite my better judgement, I made my way to the bars and looked up and down to find the source of the voice. A man with a stick which looked like what I imagined a magic wand would look like stood two rooms down from mine.

"Quickly," he said.

The skinny man chuckled. "He never has learned good manners. I should teach him, but I think it'd be a lost cause."

I rolled my eyes. What good was that supposed to do me?

Eventually, someone stuck their arm through the bars. The man pressed the magic wand against their skin. There was a sharp yelp of pain, then he pulled it back.

"Red. Let her go," he instructed.

"I'll be back," the skinny man said, sidling down the hall with a set of keys clanking at his waist.

Was it really as simple as that? They'd test me for this blood they thought I might have, and then when I didn't, I'd be able to go home. Though that would cause another problem in that I had no idea where *home* was from here.

I slipped my hand into my pocket and felt around for the key to the tower. I relaxed slightly when my fingers closed around it. It was too small to be any use in an escape attempt, but it was reassuring that they hadn't taken it from me. If I could get back to the village, and couldn't find Archie, then at least I could return to my own bed.

The man with the magic wand had moved on to the cell next to mine. I wondered why they were doing this? What did Silver Blood do?

He repeated the process, sticking the wand into the girl's arm until she yelped.

"Red," he grunted. "Let her go."

The skinny man hurried over, but I didn't pay

any attention. I couldn't when I knew it was going to be my turn next.

"Arm," the man demanded.

"You shouldn't bother. My blood is red," I pointed out. I'd cut myself often enough over the years to be certain about that.

The man laughed, the sound booming around the room. "That's not how Silver Blood works."

I frowned. Then why was it called that? If something was named after a colour, then I'd have expected it to look that way too.

"Arm," he repeated brusquely.

With nothing else for it, I stuck my arm through the bars and waited for him to prick me. He didn't waste any time and pressed the wand down into my flesh. I winced, but didn't cry out. It didn't hurt as much as I thought it would.

He pulled the wand back and his eyebrow raised. "Silver."

Huh. That made no sense. I looked down at my arm, but there was nothing more than a red droplet where the wand had pricked me. There certainly wasn't anything silver about it. Not even a sparkle.

"I don't understand..." I started, but the man was already gone, quickly replaced by the skinny man once more.

"Ah, you're one of the ones who didn't know about your blood. Don't worry about it. Not everyone does," he explained.

Kind of. I'd call his explanation somewhat lacking.

"What happens now?" I asked. That was the more immediate issue. I could deal with the Silver Blood thing later.

"You follow me." He slipped the key into the lock and undid it. The bars swung open.

I stepped out, glancing either way to take stock of the situation. Unfortunately for me, there were several guards at either end. I guessed that was all I needed to see to know I wasn't going to be able to make a break for it. Instead, I followed the skinny man, hoping he'd give me a clue into what was going on.

If I played along, I might get a chance to escape and run back to the village. And to Archie.

Please wait for me. I knew there was no way Archie would be able to hear or otherwise receive my message, but it comforted me to think about him.

To my surprise, the skinny man led me into a plush room with racks of dresses and comfortable looking chairs which made me want to sit in them.

What was happening here? None of it made any sense.

"Have a seat," he instructed, pointing me towards one of the chairs.

I glanced at the door in time to see a guard close it. There was no getting away from what was happening that way, then. So much for that.

"What's going on?" I asked as I took a seat. If there was no chance of escape yet, then there was no reason for me to be uncomfortable.

I straightened out my skirts, grimacing as I discovered a tear in them. I shouldn't be surprised. I'd been manhandled at various points and had fallen on the forest floor. But it would be a pain to try and explain how I'd damaged it to Mother.

If I got back to the tower before she did anyway. If I didn't, then it would be a moot point. Though perhaps I could try and claim I'd been kidnapped straight from the tower.

"You've been found to have Silver Blood," the skinny man said. "That means you're to be escorted to the palace..."

"What?" I blurted.

"...Where you will be entitled to take part in the competition which will choose the Crown Prince's wife," he continued without acknowledging my question.

"I don't want to be his wife," I countered quickly. "I want to go home."

"Unfortunately, that is not possible," the skinny man replied.

"Why not? I don't want to go to the palace, and you can't make me," I pointed out.

"You will, and we can. As you have Silver Blood, you are therefore a possession of the state. As we are aware of your existence, we are required to send you to the palace for the competition."

"But what is this Silver Blood?" And why hadn't I ever heard of it? I'd never noticed anything special about my blood. It was just... well, blood. Neither had Mother, for that matter. Though I supposed if she was aware of the situation, perhaps it explained why she'd kept me away from the world.

"There is power in Silver Blood, girl. Remember that."

I scowled. Wasn't he going to tell me anything useful? I supposed in his mind, informing me that I was going to the palace and going to compete to be someone's wife was useful information, despite the fact I didn't *want* any of that. Archie was the one I wanted. I should have said yes to him last night, and then none of this would have happened.

The skinny man didn't give any consideration to my mood and walked across to the rail of dresses.

He searched among them, though I wasn't sure for what.

I simply seethed. I wasn't about to make things easier for him if I didn't have to. He'd made it very clear I was a captive here, and I wasn't about to start thinking I wasn't.

"I think this one is the one for you." He pulled a green gown from the rail and held it up for me.

"A dress?" My shock came through despite the fact I was trying to act as if I was uninterested.

"You can't turn up at the palace like you are now. You look as if you were pulled through a hedge backwards."

"I was," I muttered under my breath. What did he expect when I'd been chased through a forest, kidnapped, thrown in a dirty cell, and prodded with a magic wand that told me what colour my blood was? He wouldn't look like sunshine and roses in those circumstances either.

"You'll be taken through to the bathing chambers by one of the maids..."

There were maids here? Other than the women in the cells, I hadn't seen any others. Perhaps they were simply hiding from the people who'd been locked up.

"They'll see to your toilette and clothing. Guards

will be behind every door. Don't think you can escape your fate," he warned.

I rolled my eyes, well aware of what he was trying to do. I wasn't about to let myself be intimidated by him. No matter what happened, I would stand up straight and face it head-on. I could do this.

"And after that?" I prompted.

"You'll be taken to the palace. And the competition will begin."

"And what do you get out of that?"

He laughed. "Nothing. I'm simply doing my job."

"It's your job to kidnap people from their homes and prod them?"

"No. It's my job to find people with Silver Blood. I have nothing to do with any kidnap," he said as he placed the dress on a separate rail and started sorting through a box of accessories.

I crossed my arms. "Then I'm allowed to write home?" I wasn't sure what I was going to say. Or who I'd send it to. But it felt right to at least try.

He shrugged. "Sure. If you know the name of where you live."

My heart sank. I had no idea. I'd only ever thought of it as the *village*, which was problematic when it came to sending a message. I was going to have to find another way.

"From your expression, I take it you don't. In

which case, just go with it. Accept your fate and do your duty."

I narrowed my eyes. Who did he think he was telling me all of this? I didn't *want* to be a princess. I didn't even want to go to the palace. And yet, that was what was going to happen next. Whether I liked it or not, apparently.

CHAPTER FIVE

THE GUARD at my back made it hard to enjoy the walk through the palace. I knew I *technically* wasn't supposed to like it at all, given that I'd been taken from my life, put in a pretty dress, and made to come here, but it was hard not to find it beautiful. Every time we turned a corner, there was another exquisite piece of art or someone playing music without missing a single note. It was magical in a way I'd never experienced before.

A small part of me wanted to stay simply for this. The rest of me knew I had to get back to where I'd come from, even if it would take me a long time to even figure out where that was. Mother would be back in the morning and discover me gone, and I had no idea what she'd do. Could she find me at the palace? I wasn't sure. We hadn't travelled for more than an hour between the cells and the palace, but I had no idea how far I'd come the night before.

But ultimately, it did mean I couldn't be *too* far away from home.

At least, I hoped that was the case. And that Archie wouldn't give up on me just because I wasn't there this morning. I hated the idea of him thinking I'd abandoned him when I should have said yes. With everything that had gone on, I hadn't even made a decision about that. But my instincts were telling me that I should hold on tight to him and never let him go.

So long as I could find him again.

Perhaps he was even at the palace. He'd talked about his parents pressuring him to marry. That was mostly a noble thing. And if he was trying to find a wife, then the royal court would be the place to do it. My heart lifted at the thought. Perhaps I'd run into him here and everything else would no longer matter. He could even help me get a message to Mother, though I wasn't sure what it would say.

"We're here," my guard grumbled, pushing on a door and waiting for me to step inside.

Was he going to follow me around the palace for the entire competition? I didn't think that would go down very well. Nor would it look good. Perhaps he was only going to stay until he was sure I wasn't going to run away. I should tell him that I wasn't going to until I was certain Archie wasn't here. I knew it was a long shot, but I had to hold out hope that it would be the case. It was the only way out of this situation that didn't fill me with dread.

I entered the room and did a double-take as I realised there was another woman in it.

"Hello," I said, finding my voice. There was no reason for me to be rude to her. Far from it. Perhaps she'd have some of the answers I needed.

"Hi," she responded brightly, bouncing out of her seat and rushing towards me. "I'm Rosemary." She held out her hand.

I was about to take it when she dropped it.

"I'm sorry, I forgot I'm not supposed to do that any more."

"Why not?" I asked with a frown. It seemed like a good way to greet someone. I'd seen many of the villagers use the gesture as they went about their day.

She cocked her head to the side and looked me up and down. "You're not noble, are you?"

"Not unless there's someone in my family history I don't know about," I admitted.

"Me neither. Why don't you come sit down? We have tea we can drink." She ushered me over to a small table laden with tea and cakes.

Seeing nothing else for it, I sat down in one of the chairs. I was already a little frustrated with myself for being complacent with everything going on, so it wouldn't do any harm if I went with the flow now.

My guard crossed his arms, standing just inside the doorway.

"You only just got here, then?" Rosemary asked, nodding towards the man.

I nodded, not seeing any problem with admitting it to her. My guard was making everything pretty obvious, whether I wanted him to or not.

"What's your name?" she asked. "I can't keep thinking about you as the new blonde girl."

I chuckled. "Cosette."

"It's good to meet you," Rosemary said.

"You too." Could I ask her about what was going on? Would she tell me?

"You can ask me anything you want," she assured me. "Even if it feels like something you should know already."

A nervous laugh escaped me. "Is it that obvious?"

She shrugged. "Not to everyone. But I've only been here a few days. I haven't forgotten how crazy it all feels at the beginning."

"I don't even know what I'm doing here," I admitted. "They keep saying it's some kind of competition to marry the prince..." I trailed off, hoping she could fill in some of the gaps.

"That's pretty much all there is to it. From what I've heard, there are five tests. And a ball tonight. But I don't know much more than that. The other girls don't like to talk to me much. I think that's why they had me wait for you here."

"You don't mind that?"

"Why would I mind? I'd rather talk to someone like you who will have interesting things to say than some of the vapid ninnies you'll meet later. You'd think they've never done anything interesting in their lives."

A weak smile spread over my face. I had no idea how to respond to that comment when I hadn't met them.

"What about the nobles not in the competition? Will we get to meet them at the ball?" I asked, trying not to get my hopes up. If it was tonight, then perhaps I'd get a chance to see Archie sooner than I thought. If he was here. I had to try and remember that he might not be at court. Or a noble. He could simply be a farmer's son. Though it seemed unlikely given the amount of money he always had, and the quality of his clothes. Neither of those things had even crossed my mind as relevant until now.

"Most of them, I assume. But I don't know.

They've kept me separate while they tried to teach me some of the rules." Rosemary grimaced. "You should drink some tea while it's warm. If you don't, it'll get bitter and that isn't so nice."

I poured myself a cup, topped up hers, and splashed in a dash of milk. I eyed the sugar cubes warily, unsure if I wanted to try one. Mother had them in her own drinks from time to time, but hadn't allowed me to. The last thing I wanted was to ruin my tea by putting one in case I wouldn't actually like it.

I decided against it. I could try it at a later point. If I stayed here longer than a day.

"How will the competition work?" I asked.

"They'll give us tasks to do, and we'll be judged based on how we perform. I think some girls are sent home between each round, until only one is left and she becomes the next queen."

"How many girls *are* there?" I asked, my eyes widening.

"I didn't count," Rosemary admitted, then took a sip of her tea.

I lifted mine to my mouth and blew across the top. The scent of it tickled my nose, and I had to stop and breathe more of it in. It was better than the leaves we had at home. What a nice treat.

I took a sip.

It tasted better than the tea we had at home too. I didn't know if it was the leaves themselves, or the milk which tasted better.

"Did you say there was a ball tonight?" I asked, knowing full well that she had. I simply wanted to get her back on the subject.

"Yes. It's supposed to be to celebrate the start of the competition."

"Are we going to have to dance?" I tried to keep the horror out of my voice. I knew some basic barn dances from when I'd first started sneaking into the village, but not how to properly dance the way people at court did it. I was certain I'd make a fool out of myself if I tried.

A small part of me worried that the ball was some kind of test in itself, but I pushed it away. What did it matter if it was? I wanted to be there to find out if Archie was here. I didn't need to stick around any longer than that. If he was at the ball, then I could leave tomorrow with him. If he wasn't, there were worse things that could happen than me being sent home.

Though who knew if they'd let me do that considering I had this mythical Silver Blood. I didn't even know what the excitement about that was.

Should I ask Rosemary? She seemed to know a lot of stuff. Perhaps she knew something about

Silver Blood too? But then, what if she didn't and stopped wanting to talk to me? I wasn't naive enough to think the other women would welcome me with open arms considering where I'd come from.

"I don't know," she said, reminding me that I'd asked her about dancing. "But I hope it isn't too complicated, or I'll never pick it up in time."

"Do you think they'll teach us how to do it first?"

She shook her head. "Not a chance. They don't want a commoner to actually *win*. We're just here to make it look like someone of low birth stands a chance at being the next Queen. It's all about how it looks."

"Ah." It made sense. But then, why me? Couldn't they have left me to my quiet country life and not dragged me to a palace far from home?

Before I could ask any other questions, the door opened, startling my guard.

I tried not to laugh at his jumpiness, but a small one escaped anyway. It was good finally seeing him having things a little bit harder.

"My Ladies," a servant said, bowing deeply to the two of us.

I exchanged a confused glance with Rosemary, grateful to see that she was equally as unfamiliar with the gesture.

"Is everything all right?" I asked.

"Of course, my lady. But they're ready for you in the reception room. Please, follow me," he said.

I exchanged another glance with Rosemary. She shrugged and set down her teacup. I did the same and rose to my feet. It sounded like my entire day was going to be one thing after another.

I hoped I'd get somewhere nice to sleep tonight. I was going to need it.

CHAPTER SIX

It was impossible to ignore the way the noble ladies looked at us. They clearly thought we weren't worth their time, though none of them would outright say it. I supposed that made sense. They were brought up to be polite and dignified, and we were here encroaching on their territory.

I resisted the urge to step closer to Rosemary. In this situation, there probably wasn't much safety in numbers. Especially not when there were only two of us.

"What is *she* doing here?" The woman turned up her nose as she looked down on me. I wasn't sure why *I* was being singled out when Rosemary came from non-noble stock too.

"They say she has Silver Blood," the one to her left responded.

I tried not to feel dowdy next to them in my clearly inferior gown. But there was something off putting about them both. These women had something I didn't, and potentially never would.

But I needed to be kind to myself. I hadn't asked to be here. Nor had there been any time to prepare for what I was going to face. I'd never even *met* women like this before.

"Silver Blood." The first woman tutted loudly. "I don't know why they let them compete."

"It's not like I was given a choice," I muttered.

"Why are you talking to me?" the woman spat out. "No one gave you permission to speak."

"She doesn't need permission," Rosemary interrupted, stepping up beside me.

"Nobody asked you." The woman glared at the two of us.

"And nobody made you the Princess," Rosemary responded. "So you don't get to boss us about."

"Not yet, anyway."

I bit my lip, trying not to give this woman a piece of my mind. I knew that wouldn't get me anywhere other than more hated by her, though at this rate, she wasn't going to change her mind on how she felt about me. Despite the fact we hadn't even been properly introduced. Some people would never change their minds about anything, and she was that type.

The woman flounced away, leaving me standing there with Rosemary.

"Don't let Rebekah get to you. From what I've seen over the past few days, she's like that with everyone."

"Holier than thou?" I asked.

Rosemary giggled. "Exactly."

"Can I ask you something?" Even as the words slipped out, I wondered if I should risk it.

"Of course."

"Why are you here?" Perhaps I shouldn't have asked. But it would be nice to know something about my ally that wasn't just her name.

"I imagine for the same reason you are," she answered cryptically. "They said you had Silver Blood."

"Apparently. But I don't know anything about it," I admitted. It might be crazy to trust this woman, but the words were coming out of my mouth faster than I wanted them to.

She shrugged. "You're not going to like it, but the honest answer is that there's nothing to it, really. Legends say that those who were born with Silver Blood often became mages and wizards, maybe even hedge witches. But it's been watered down over the years until people can't even tell if they have it without special testing equipment."

I frowned, never having heard stories about it at all. Though that shouldn't be a surprise. Mother had kept me away from the world for the most part, and it was only in the past couple of years that I'd started sneaking out. Even then, I'd been more focused on keeping to myself, and a little later, to only Archie and myself.

"How do you know all this?" I asked.

"My family used to be the mage type of Silver Blood. The stories got passed down the generations until they got to me."

"So you weren't caught and brought here?"

"Of course not," Rosemary assured me quickly. "The call was made about the competition, and as a Silver Blood, I'm entitled to my place. I offered to come. Didn't you?"

I was about to answer when a loud thumping caught our attention.

"Attention everyone," a man's voice boomed out and the chattering of the women died down as a result.

Interesting, there was some kind of order here. That was good to know.

"As you know, you are here to compete for the hand of the Crown Prince. You're lucky to have been born in the age you have, otherwise, you would have missed out on this amazing chance."

That was all the women needed to start chattering again. I tried to avoid rolling my eyes, but even so, I was grateful no one was watching me too closely.

"You'll each be put through a series of tasks. If you aren't awarded over a certain amount of points per round, then you will be disqualified and sent back to your home in disgrace. Should multiple ladies make it to the final round, one additional test will be put forward."

"There'll be no need for that," Rebekah announced loudly. "I'll be the victor."

"That well may be Lady Fynes, but the law states that all eligible Ladies and Silvers are given a chance to participate," the announcer said.

"That's us," Rosemary whispered to me.

"Are we the only ones?"

"As far as I know," she responded. "But perhaps some of the ladies have the Blood too but are choosing to keep it quiet. I suspect it would somehow diminish their status if they were seen to be at the same level as us."

I grimaced. That hardly seemed fair.

"When does the first test begin?" Rebekah demanded.

The man ignored her. He must have been used to women like her demanding a lot from him, as he didn't even flinch away.

"There will be a ball this evening..." he continued.

"I don't have anything to wear," I whispered hastily to Rosemary.

"There'll be things in your room," she replied, sticking her hand in front of her mouth so no one could see us talking.

"Oh."

"You have no idea what's going on, do you?" she asked.

A woman in front of us twisted around and shushed us.

I suppressed a giggle. How had this become my life? All I'd been doing was trying to return home so I could think over Archie's proposal. Except that there was nothing to think about now. Part of my hesitation had been in not wanting Mother to know I'd disappeared. With the way things were going, it didn't seem likely she *wouldn't* learn about my jaunt out of the tower, no matter how much I tried to avoid her learning.

"No," I replied, though I suspected too much time had passed for her to pick the conversation back up.

The room was heating up, and the mingling

scents of all the women's perfumes was starting to make my head pinch.

"You're expected to wear the appropriate attire for each event, no matter if that is breakfast, lunch, dinner, or the ball this evening. If at any point, your comportment is deemed to be unworthy, then it could lead to instant dismissal from the competition."

Panic bloomed inside me. How was I going to manage that? I knew I was only trying to make it to the ball tonight so I could look for Archie, but there was still a lot of time between then and now, and the last thing I needed was to be sent home early.

Especially when I had no idea where *home* actually was. And that wasn't even in a figurative way, though I was aware that question was up for debate as much as some of the others.

Rosemary laid a hand on my arm. "You need to calm down," she whispered. "The others will notice."

"I..." My word trailed off as I realised I had no idea what was supposed to follow it. Should I admit that I didn't know anything about dressing right? Or acting the correct way? I didn't even know how to curtsy. And from the way the servants had treated me since I'd arrived, that was something I'd need to learn how to do.

"We can go through all of it, but not until we're out of here."

"How do you even know all of this?" Tears pricked at the corners of my eyes, but I blinked them away. Rosemary was right about that. I couldn't show weakness of any kind or the others here would pounce on it.

"You're all dismissed," the man announced. "You're expected at six for dinner."

The room dissolved back into the chatter of the various women. From what I could see, a lot of them must have known one another already, leaving both Rosemary and I excluded.

"Come on," she said, tugging at my sleeve. "We can find out what room is yours and go through all the things you need to know."

"You still haven't told me how *you* know them," I pointed out, but still went with her.

My guard pushed away from the wall and fell into step behind us. I hadn't even realised the man was still following me, but I supposed it did make sense. I wasn't completely done being a flight risk in most people's eyes.

"I've been preparing for this most of my life," she responded. "As soon as Mother found out I was the same age as the Prince, she knew this might happen and didn't want me to be behind the other girls, even if I wasn't noble."

"Oh." So it was only me at a disadvantage.

I supposed that would have mattered a great deal more if I'd been trying to win the Prince myself.

CHAPTER SEVEN

The banquet hall was noisier than I expected. I smoothed down the skirts of yet another unfamiliar dress. None of the clothing that had been waiting for me in the room they'd assigned was recognisable to me. I hadn't enough experience when it came to clothes.

Thankfully, Rosemary seemed to be more clued in than I was, and had instructed me on what to wear for each event and time of day. It had briefly crossed my mind she could be trying to sabotage me by telling me the wrong information, but I found that unlikely. Each time she'd told me what a dress was for, and how I should have the maids do my hair to match, it clicked in my mind and made sense. A ball gown wasn't suitable for a dinner where I had to sit, but a day dress wasn't fancy enough to make a statement.

Getting into the clothes was another matter, but the maids had been patient with me while putting me into the dress I'd requested.

I scanned the room, searching for someone I recognised. At first, I thought it was Rosemary I was looking for, but after another moment, I realised I was hoping Archie would be here already around and I could skip the rest of the evening.

Unfortunately, it seemed that this meal was only for those of us who were part of this stupid competition.

I spied an empty seat, and almost sighed with relief when I noticed Rosemary in the one next to it. At least I wouldn't have to eat my dinner in silence while stuck between two women who hated my mere existence.

All I had to do was get through this meal without drawing too much attention to myself, and the ball would be within my grasp. Then I could find Archie.

I pushed away the idea that I was wrong about him and he wasn't noble. He *had* to be at the ball. If he wasn't then I had no idea what I was going to do. If I spent more time in the competition, perhaps I could learn more about my Silver Blood. It might hold the answer to how I could support myself without Mother's help. It seemed silly to think the solution to a problem I'd had my entire life could have been in my veins.

But right now, I didn't have enough information to know for sure.

I moved through the room, being careful to walk at a steady pace so I didn't fall over in the small heels I was wearing. Not through choice, but the man's voice from earlier was still ringing in my ears. If I wasn't wearing the right thing, then I'd be removed from the competition no matter what stage it was at. I didn't see him in the room right now, but that didn't mean anything. For all I knew, one of the many women sat around was reporting to him.

I took my seat, making sure to spread out my skirts so they fell right. Or as right as I thought they should. As foreign as it was, I loved the dress. The fabric was finer than anything I'd ever come across in my life, and it fit me perfectly, though I had no idea why. Perhaps it was something to do with magic. More likely, they'd taken my measurements while I was unconscious last night. That wasn't the nicest thought, but I supposed it could be worse. Saying that, I still had a huge gap in what happened, and not a lot of explanation.

No one talked much as the first few courses were served, so I took my time, watching the other women to see which utensil they used to eat with. I didn't recognise half of them, but no one seemed to notice me watching, and I was careful to react quickly so that didn't change.

"You may as well all go home," Rebekah announced loudly as they were serving dessert.

It was the first time anyone had spoken loud enough for anyone they weren't in a conversation to hear.

"And why would that be?" another girl asked, arching a perfectly groomed eyebrow.

"I'm going to win."

"I think Felicia has more of a chance than you do," the first girl responded.

Not having any clue what was going on, I leaned into Rosemary. "Who is Felicia?"

She nodded to a beautiful brunette sitting three seats down and across the table. "I've heard that she's the Prince's childhood sweetheart," she whispered.

"Oh don't be so foolish, Gertrude," Rebekah snapped. "Everyone knows the two of them haven't been together in a long time."

Gertrude got to her feet, scraping her chair back loudly and calling everyone's attention to the situation. As if anyone wasn't already watching with a keen interest. This was the kind of thing I *hadn't* expected to happen when I'd been told I was part of this.

"What do you know, Rebekah?" she spat out. "You're nothing more than a social-climbing gossip who doesn't know when to stop. Don't think we all don't know what you did to get here."

My eyes widened, but I didn't ask Rosemary about what the words meant. I didn't care that much, but also, it seemed in bad taste to gossip about someone who was in the room with us still.

Rebekah's cheeks flamed red. No doubt that meant there was some truth in Gertrude's words, even if I didn't have any idea what it was.

"Ah-hem."

Our attention flitted from the almost-fight between Gertrude and Rebekah, to the woman who was now sitting at the head of the table with a serious expression on her face.

"Good evening, ladies. Welcome to the most important competition of your life."

A hush sounded as what was happening hit everyone. This was all part of it.

"You may not have realised it, but this dinner was your first test."

Whispers sounded behind me as a couple of the girls talked to one another about what that meant.

Dread sank to the pit of my stomach as I thought

about everything I'd done and said since the beginning of the meal. As far as I could tell, I hadn't done anything wrong. But I had no idea how to do any of it right to begin with to be able to tell for sure. What if I'd used the wrong spoon to eat my sorbet? Or what if asking who Felicia was had made a mistake?

"Lady Gertrude Stonefall," the woman said.

Gertrude swayed from side to side, not having retaken her seat since she got up to accuse Rebekah. She opened her mouth as if to speak, but the words fell away.

"Please leave the room. You'll be escorted out of the palace by the guards. You are expected to return to your home and not speak about any of the other participants," the woman said.

A part of me expected the other girls to say something about it, even if it was just to gossip among themselves. But that wasn't the case. Silence rang out through the room.

Gertrude reddened as the embarrassment took hold. She composed herself quickly, stepping back and dipping into an elegant curtsy aimed at the woman in question.

"Thank you for allowing me to take part." Her voice wobbled as she threatened to burst into tears.

I longed to jump to my feet and rush over to comfort her, despite the fact we didn't know one another. I resisted, not wanting to draw any attention to myself. I still had a ball to get to, and hopefully, Archie to find. And I wasn't certain I could help Gertrude anyway.

I turned my attention to Rebekah, who was leaning back in her chair with a smug smile stretching over her lips. She was over the moon to have provoked a girl until she'd gotten kicked out.

It didn't even matter that I didn't know Gertrude. I hated Rebekah for it. She was clearly the kind of woman who took pleasure in bringing others down, and I didn't have time for people like that.

Gertrude's skirts rustled as she moved through the room. Her pale pink gown swished along the floor, and even though she was leaving, I found myself studying her movements. I could walk like that, if I tried. I probably wouldn't look quite as elegant, but I had to at least try.

The doors clanged shut the moment she was out of them, and I found a shiver heading down my spine. It was almost too easy to get booted out. I didn't like that at all.

"Congratulations to the rest of you," the woman at the head of the table said, pulling my attention back to her. "You've passed the first test. Please, get some rest before the ball. I expect you all to be looking your best when the time comes." She rose to her feet and then gestured for one of the other guards to follow her.

I scanned the other assembled men, searching for my own guard, but I couldn't find him. Perhaps he'd finally returned to the cells where they'd kept me last night. Or he might be waiting outside for me to exit.

The moment the woman was out of the room, the assembled women started chattering away.

"Did you realise this was a test?" one of them asked, voicing the same question the rest of us had.

"I guessed," Rebekah answered loudly, earning an eye roll from the questioner.

"Who was the woman?" I whispered to Rosemary, not wanting any of the others to hear in case it was a stupid question to ask.

She shrugged. "Some kind of royal aid? I don't know, I haven't been here long enough."

"I guess we'll find out eventually," I responded, then reached out for my wine glass.

I hadn't drunk much of it over the course of the meal, but now my stomach was full, it didn't seem like too much of a risk.

The tart liquid hit my tongue, both sweet and sour at the same time. There was no way I could drink a lot of this, though some of the other women disagreed.

"Do you want help deciding what to wear for the ball?" Rosemary whispered to me.

"You just want to get out of here," I teased.

"Definitely. Now that woman is gone, there's nothing stopping Rebekah from ripping us all to shreds."

I smothered a laugh, not wanting to draw too much attention to us given the subject of our conversation.

"You're right there."

"Then let's go. It'll take us twice as long to get ready as everyone else," she joked.

I nodded my agreement. She was right. There were so many buttons and ribbons on the clothes we were wearing, that it took even longer than normal to get dressed, especially when I had to learn what went whereas I dressed. The maids were there to help, but I'd only let them do so much.

"Plus, there's my hair," I agreed. At the moment, it was tied back in a plait down my back. I loved the way it looked and felt when it was like that. But somehow, I didn't think it would be deemed acceptable for an event like the ball.

CHAPTER EIGHT

THE ROOM WAS FILLED with explosions of colour and the excited chatter of the maids. It was almost impossible to think about anything.

Or move. But that was mostly due to the number of pins in my dress. While they'd managed to get a dress fitted for me that I could wear at dinner, they hadn't managed to finish the ball gown. I wasn't too surprised. I had appeared rather abruptly.

"Do they give all of the girls wardrobes like this?" I asked Rosemary, who had somehow convinced her maids to let her get ready in the same room as me. Her dress was already fitted, though, so it was taking less time to get her ready.

"I don't think so," she admitted. "They do it for us so that it levels the playing field and people don't judge us for being lower class."

"Pfft." The noise escaped unbidden, but I didn't regret it.

"I know. It's ridiculous. Everyone knows who we are, and they look down on us for it. At least, most of them do." An unmistakable twinge of sadness entered her voice. Perhaps the situation got to her more than she wanted to admit. I supposed it had to if she'd been focusing on studying for this her entire life because of her blood.

I tried to imagine something similar. Though I supposed my own upbringing had been similarly strange considering I'd spent my life in a tower. Did Mother know about my Silver Blood? Was that why she'd kept me away from everyone else? To me, that made no sense, especially not if no one could actually *tell* from the outside. And I assumed not, or they wouldn't have to prod people with the magic wand.

"Please lift your arms, Miss," one of the maids said. She seemed to be in charge of this part of the process, so perhaps she was a seamstress instead of a serving girl. I had no way of knowing. The only thing I was certain of when it came to them was that they probably came from a higher station in life than I did.

I stretched my arms out and waited for her to do her thing. Unable to help myself, I sucked in a breath as she stuck a pin in the sleeve. Not that she caught my skin. The only indication she'd even done anything was that the fabric tightened around my arm, constricting, but not hurting.

"Your wardrobe is provided to give you the best chance at participating in the competition," the seamstress-maid said. "It's an option offered to any of the ladies competing whose families don't have the means. There are three of you taking advantage of the offer this year."

I exchanged a glance with Rosemary. It hadn't occurred to me someone else might be at a similar disadvantage to us. I had no idea who it could be as all of the others seemed far better off than the two of us did.

The seamstress didn't say anything else as she sewed up the sleeve. I'd prefer it if she didn't do this kind of thing while I was *in* the dress, but the ball started in an hour, so it didn't seem like the best time to start complaining about it. I had to look my best, or they might send me away before I got into the ballroom at all.

"Are you looking forward to the dance?" I asked Rosemary.

"Oh yes, it'll be wonderful. Have you ever been to one before?"

I shook my head. "Have you?"

She nodded. "Once. It was a harvest festival, and

the people in the surrounding villages were invited too. Mother put me into my best dress and paraded me around. I think she was hoping I'd catch the eye of a nobles who would take a liking to me and decide I would be his wife."

"I thought they wanted you to marry the Prince," I countered.

"Oh, they do. But we all know that's not very likely given the number of girls here. Especially when they're all so much better bred than me." She shrugged, then yelped as the maid behind her accidentally tugged on her hair as a result. "Sorry," she muttered to the girls.

"You have as good a chance as anyone here," I pointed out, though I didn't believe it. Not really.

As far as I was concerned, I wouldn't last the whole night, and I was certain Rosemary knew her own fate was somewhat similar. Given the circumstances, we were lucky to be here at all.

Which was a ridiculous thing for me to think. I was here by force, and no matter how delicious the food was, or how well the dresses fit, I had to remember that. My goal was to find Archie, hope he forgave me for not turning up to meet him this morning, and then run away from here. I didn't even know if I wanted to find Mother after we left the palace. A small part of me wanted to go back and find her. The rest of me couldn't help but remember that I'd spent my entire life locked in a tower, and any time I talked about doing something outside it, she'd dismiss me and insist on there being nothing else for it.

The maids left the room all at once, though I had no idea why. They must have been up to something that didn't involve us.

"Between you and me, I'm not that interested in the Prince," Rosemary said once she was certain there was no one around.

"Is this where I'm supposed to be shocked?" I joked.

A light laugh escaped from her. "Of all the people here, you're probably the only one who could possibly understand," she admitted.

She walked over to the looking glass and tapped the side of her hair lightly as she tried to work out what the maids had done.

"It's a surreal situation, that's for sure," I muttered.

"Exactly. And a Prince feels too high for the likes of us. How could we ever keep up with him anyway? We'd have to learn all of the court rules and regulations, while starting a new relationship, and having to do all the things a princess should." She shrugged. "It's not for me."

"I thought you'd been studying the rules and regulations your whole life?" I picked up my skirt and stepped down from the podium the seamstress had made me stand on. As far as I could tell, she'd finished with me, and I didn't think there were any pins nestled in the fabric any more. That wouldn't stop me from being extra careful as I moved around for the next couple of hours. No doubt the care would fade once I was at the ball.

"The ones I can learn, sure. But there are dozens of unspoken rules and points of etiquette that we have no idea about because we weren't *born* to it."

"Oh." I shouldn't be surprised by that. I'd learned a lot in the past day, including a lot I hadn't had a clue about beforehand.

"But let's not worry about it for now." She turned around and held out a hand to me.

I took it, despite being rather confused by the whole situation.

"We should make the most of the opportunity we do have," she informed me. "Which includes having as much fun as we can, for as long as we can."

I grinned in response. I should tell her about my plan to find Archie, but somehow, I felt as if it would destroy this moment.

"All right, then. Let's go to the ball," I said instead.

CHAPTER NINE

It was almost impossible not to stand in the middle of the room with my mouth open. There was so much colour and movement in the room, and I couldn't find the words to process it all. I'd read about balls and royal functions in books growing up, but nothing had prepared me for this.

I glanced to my side to see how Rosemary was taking it, but the girl had disappeared already. Where could she have gone? Had someone whisked her onto the dance floor already? If so, that must have meant our status wasn't well known here.

A pang of loss ran through me as I realised I'd have to experience the ball without my new friend by my side. But then, it would make it all the easier to search for Archie among the faces of the elite.

Would he recognise me? My hair was distinctive,

but the way the maids had styled it might make the length more difficult to make out. And what about him? He'd be dressed differently in order to blend in with the other nobles too. From what I'd seen so far, that meant a lot of colour and embellishments I wasn't used to seeing him in. What if I walked straight past him and didn't even realise?

I pushed aside that thought. I'd know him. He was the only person who'd ever held my heart. If I came face to face with him, there'd be no doubts in my mind.

A serving man approached with a tray of wine, but I waved him away. The glass from dinner had been enough, especially as there was another test tomorrow, if the whispers of the maids were to be believed. I wished whoever was running this whole thing would be more upfront with us all. Or perhaps they were being, but were skipping me and Rosemary to put us at a disadvantage. They might have been obliged to let us be part of the competition, but I doubted there was anything in the rules that stated they had to make it *easy* for us.

Trumpets blared, and everything stopped, from the music to the dancing. People parted, making way for whoever it was being announced.

"His Majesty, King Rupert, Her Majesty, Queen Diane, His Highness, the Crown Prince Archibald, and Her Highness, the Princess Sophie," a herald called out.

I looked on alongside everyone else as the four royals swept into the room. There was something familiar about the King's face, but I couldn't put my finger on what. Perhaps there'd been a poster with it up in the village at some point.

The Queen was a sight to be seen. If I thought the noblewomen had been dressed beautifully, then the royal women showed me something completely different. Their dresses dripped with opulent fabrics and glittering jewels, perfectly balanced to look stunning, and not gaudy.

But all of that paled in significance when my gaze landed on the Prince.

Archie.

He was at the ball after all, but he wasn't a noble.

It all made sense. The King seemed familiar because the two of them shared a nose. And a smile. Archie was short for Archibald, which I should have figured out myself, but I'd been too busy wondering how I'd manage to find him.

He'd said his parents were pressuring him to find a wife. If I'd come away with him, perhaps I wouldn't have had to go through this entire competition. Then again, maybe I would have.

One thing was for certain, I no longer wanted to

leave the competition after the ball was over. I planned on seeing this whole thing out.

Archie's gaze landed on mine, and his whole demeanour changed. His eyes lit up, and his shoulders stopped slumping. I hadn't even realised he was slouching until that moment.

"Wait for me," he mouthed at me.

I nodded, my heart feeling so much lighter just from seeing him. It was silly, really. But then, I had been looking for him. It made sense that finding him had this effect on me.

The four royals took their places in front of the thrones against the back wall of the ballroom. The assembled people all turned to watch them. Not that I needed their cue to do so. My gaze was fixated on Archie, the same as his kept flickering back to me.

"Welcome," the King boomed, his voice filled with command only his station could bring him. "I hope you enjoy the opening ball to my son's marriage competition. As you may know, he will dance with each of the eligible ladies. They will be tested over the next week, and at the end of it, one of them will become my son's fiancée."

Voices rose around the room as people began to compare notes on the women. Oh. Wait. I was one of them. Though most of the people here probably had no idea I was. It was a shame there wasn't something helpful like a list with all the names on it. They'd mean nothing to me, though I was certain they would to others. Perhaps to Rosemary. Despite not being here long, she had a good grasp on what was going on.

"Prince Archibald," the King said loudly, calling my attention back to him. "Please choose one of the lovely ladies to open the dancing with."

His face lit up, and he stepped away from his throne, heading straight towards me. Should I signal that he shouldn't? I had no idea how to do any of the dances he'd want to perform, but did that matter? I wanted to spend time with him far too badly to worry about making a fool of myself.

Before I had time to decide, and mostly because I didn't seem able to make up my mind, he was right in front of me, bowing deeply.

"Lady Cosette, would you do me the honours of the first dance?" he asked, his voice low and promising.

A snort of derision sounded from behind me. No doubt it was Rebekah, though without her saying anything, I had no way of knowing. It wasn't like I was going to turn around and check right now.

Instead, I reached out and placed my hand in Archie's outstretched one, before remembering I was supposed to curtsy. The gesture was clumsy at best, but I hoped it would give me an odd kind of rustic charm. Perhaps I'd get points for that. If not, then I didn't stand a chance at convincing anyone except Archie that I was good enough to be the next Queen.

"I'd be honoured," I said loud enough for everyone else to hear. "I don't know the steps," I whispered to Archie.

"Follow my lead," he responded with a wink.

I bit my lip, but nodded eagerly. If he thought I could get away without knowing the proper moves, then I was going to trust him.

He gestured for the musicians to begin to play, then swept me up into his arms.

"Do you remember the first time we went to the waterfall?" he asked.

"Yes." How could I not? The sun had been shining, and the water had roared in our ears. We'd jumped into the lake for a swim, and ended up sharing our first kiss. It had been a day to remember, and one I'd cherished ever since.

"We danced on the bank," he said.

"We did." A smile stretched over my face at the memory.

The two of us began to sway back and forth as the music washed through us. It was slow and steady, almost as if the musicians already knew I couldn't dance. Perhaps they did. Someone could easily have whispered to them that I was one of the Silvers.

"Do you remember the steps?" he asked.

My eyebrows knit together as I tried to recall them. "I think so..."

"They weren't very complicated," he promised. "We can do them to this song."

"Thank you for helping cover for me."

"Always."

"And I'm sorry I wasn't there to meet you this morning. I would have been if I could have." I glanced away as the heat rose to my cheeks. I didn't normally feel this way around him, and it wasn't because I'd just found out he was a Prince, either. This was the pure embarrassment of having stood him up without meaning to.

"I know you would have. I spent as long as I could looking for you. I figured something bad must have happened..."

He guided us around a turn in the dance, and I had to admit I enjoyed the way my skirts twirled around me as he did. No wonder nobles liked balls like these so much.

"I was ambushed on the way back home," I admitted. "And then I was taken to some kind of holding cells, which was where I ended up this morning. They tested my blood and said I was a Silver, and then I ended up here." Wow, it seemed crazy when I said it like that. Somehow, it had felt like so much more had happened in that time. And yet, it hadn't.

Archie's eyebrows shot up. "You have Silver Blood?"

"Apparently." I shrugged. "But I have no idea what that means, or what it's used for."

"Mostly for magical objects and potions," he said. "Silvers used to be able to do magic, but not any more."

"That's a shame, or I could have magicked away my competition now I know it's you I'm competing for," I joked.

A low chuckle emitted from Archie, vibrating through me and lifting my heart. We hadn't been a part for much longer than a day, and yet being back with him made me feel so much better.

"Unfortunately, there's not much I can do about that," Archie responded. "But I can assure you you're the one I want to end this with. I was actually hoping to avoid the whole process by bringing you back."

"I'm sorry." I had to pause while Archie spun me under his arm. I let out a laugh full of freedom as I moved. "All I could think about since we parted was that I should have said yes to you as soon as you asked."

"I wish you had," he said. "But things were clearly

not meant to work out that way. And the most important thing is that you're here. Safe. And we have a chance to be together."

"So long as I can beat nineteen other women to your heart," I muttered.

Archie's expression grew serious. "There is no one else who can hold that," he promised. "Only you."

I was about to assure him of the same when someone tapped on my shoulder.

Archie stopped us from dancing, and I pulled back slightly so I could look who it was interrupting my moment with him. They better have a good reason, or I'd...do something.

My mood blackened at the sight of Rebekah waiting next to me, a smug expression on her face.

"The Prince is supposed to dance with all of us," she pointed out. "It's my turn now."

My mouth fell open, but I snapped it shut almost instantly. I didn't want her to think I was easily shocked out of behaving correctly.

Archie started to protest, but I shook my head ever so slightly until he stopped.

"That's all right," I assured him, pulling back. "Lady Rebekah." I dipped my head to her, showing her respect I certainly didn't feel. But it would be difficult for her to complain about me doing something like that without looking like a fool herself.

"I'll speak with you later, Lady Cosette," Archie said formally.

"I look forward to it, Your Highness." I dipped into a curtsy.

"She's not a lady, she's a peasant," Rebekah blurted, unable to contain herself.

"Everyone in the competition is given the status," Archie answered smoothly, hardly missing a beat. "You'd do well to remember that."

I tried not to let my amusement show, but the corners of my mouth twisted up into a smile all the same. Knowing I couldn't speak, I dipped into a curtsy and parted from the two of them. Perhaps I'd go find Rosemary. She had to resurface at some point. Whatever happened, I doubted Archie would be able to get away from the other women before the end of the night anyway. I should retire so I could be well-rested for the morning's test.

Now that the competition was underway, I doubted he'd be able to dismiss people simply because he wanted to, even if he was the one with the power. Which meant I had to prove myself at every step of the way.

And I was ready to. I'd found Archie, and now I was going to make sure I could become his Queen.

CHAPTER TEN

"Why did I drink so much last night?" one of the other women groaned. I was reasonably sure her name was Hazel, though it was hard to keep track, especially as none of them had taken the time to introduce themselves to me. I suspected they all thought I'd be gone from the competition soon, and there was no point making friends with me.

They were going to regret that once I won.

"What did I miss?" Rosemary asked as she popped up beside me.

"Depends how far back you go," I teased. "Where did you go last night?" I hadn't stayed until the end of the ball, but I had for a good while, and I hadn't seen my new friend at all in that time. I had to wonder what she'd been up to, though there was a chance she wouldn't tell me.

"I met an old friend," she admitted coyly.

I raised an eyebrow, but didn't press further. I recognised the tone in her voice, I'd used it myself when thinking about Archie. Perhaps I should have warned her that falling for someone else was risky when it came to the competition, but I doubted she needed telling that at all. She was a smart woman and one who understood the nuances of what was going on around us, even if she hadn't grown up around these women.

"You haven't missed much," I assured her, allowing her to keep her secret for now. I had to prove myself more trustworthy before she could tell me that kind of thing. "Other than a lot of complaints about hangovers."

Hazel wasn't the only one to complain. At least a dozen of the ladies surrounding us had said something of the sort.

"Has anyone been sent home?" Rosemary asked.

"Only Gertrude yesterday," a girl said from next to us. "But I suspect there will be more eliminations soon. Though it's hardly fair."

"Fair how?" I asked, scanning my memory for her name. Elizabeth, maybe? No. That wasn't right. Eliza! That was it.

She sighed. "Everyone knows the competition is rigged. It has been every time they've done it. The

Prince will be keeping a lady in, probably two, because he actually likes them, but most of the others are all to do with politics and alliances. Felicia will get to the top five because she grew up with the Prince, their families are close. Rebekah is the daughter of the army's general."

"Oh." I scanned the assembled women again, trying to work out if there was any way to tell who would be the ones who stayed, and who would go.

"You're probably safe for a little longer," Eliza said. "They want to give the masses the impression that a commoner *could* win, so they keep them around."

"What about you?" Rosemary asked.

Eliza laughed, a pretty sound which suited her heart-shaped face and dark curls. "I'll probably be gone by the end of the day," she admitted. "I don't know the Prince, I doubt he'll want to keep me around. And I'm one of the lowest-ranked people here."

"If you don't think you can win, then why are you here?" I asked, only realising how it would sound after the words had already left my mouth.

Luckily, Eliza didn't seem insulted by them. All she did was smile sadly. "I didn't have a choice. Father would have disowned me if I hadn't at least *tried.* There are better things I could be doing with my time."

"Do you gain anything by being here?" I blurted.

She cocked her head to the side. "Like what?"

"I don't know. I have no idea about any of this." I waved my hand around the room, not needing to elaborate more than that. She'd understand what I meant, especially as she'd already made the connection I was one of the commoners in the competition.

"I suppose if I got to know the Prince, then I could petition him to let women study science. I've always wanted to go to the university." She sighed wistfully. "Father would never allow it unless it had a royal seal of approval."

I sealed the information away for when I got time alone with Archie again. It didn't seem like a particularly difficult thing to do for her, especially when she was being so much nicer than all the other girls.

Someone clapped their hands, drawing our attention to the double doors in front of us. Perhaps we were about to get some kind of explanation as to why we were standing in front of the stable doors. I'd thought it was a weird place to meet, but the weather was glorious, so I hadn't worried about it too much.

"Welcome to the second day of the competition," the same man from the welcome talk said.

I perked up. This was definitely another test, then.

"For your next test, you are to enter the stables and trust your instincts. None of the creatures inside will hurt you if you approach them with the respect and care they deserve," he instructed.

I exchanged a confused glance with Rosemary and Eliza. What were we going to find inside?

Before I could think about it for too long, the doors swung open. The women began to trickle in, tentatively at first, but with more confidence when they spotted whatever was inside. I took more enjoyment than I should do at the sight of Rebekah hanging back and not seeming to want to get inside before everyone else. What was she so scared of?

With nothing else for it, I followed the others inside.

The moment I was in the stable, my jaw dropped. Was this real? I had to be imagining it. But the chatter of the women, and the interest on the faces of the small group of assembled nobles told me all I needed to know.

I really was in a stable with an assortment of creatures out of books. My gaze roved between them, trying to decide what I was supposed to do. I doubted the test was to look at the animals without touching. It was probably more to do with how we treated them up close.

A unicorn stood furthest from me, its mane shimmering in the morning light. That wasn't the creature I should approach, though. Especially because several of the other women seemed to have their eyes on it.

A loud caw sounded from above, and I glanced up to find a phoenix soaring through the rafters above us all. There was no chance of me approaching it either, though the temptation was there, especially when one of the golden feathers drifted down to the floor.

Eliza bent down and picked it up, then turned it in her fingers. She held out her arm and waited, but didn't say anything. The moment I decided to ask her what she was trying to do, the phoenix swept down and landed on her arm.

"Who is the most beautiful bird in the room?" she asked it, reaching out and smoothing down the plumage on the bird's neck. It leaned into her touch, chirping its enjoyment.

A flash of orange caught my attention, pulling it away from Eliza and the bird. It was hard to tell, as it had moved so quickly, but I was reasonably certain it had been fur.

Whatever creature it belonged to darted into one

of the stalls. I glanced over my shoulder to check no one was paying too much attention to me, and crept over to the stall. I crouched down and held out my hand, then pursed my lips and made a sound I thought would be enticing to the creature.

I was about to give up, when a slim head poked itself around the stable door. The body followed, sleek and lithe, with burnt orange fur. Its tails swayed from side to side as it walked towards me. Three of them, all standing to attention.

A kitsune. I thought they were nothing more than legends, but here was one standing in front of me.

It pushed it's head against my hand, demanding scratches. I let out a short laugh, before catching myself. The last thing I wanted to do was scare the poor creature when it was putting its trust in me.

"Hello, little one," I crooned. "What's your name?"

I knew it couldn't tell me.

No. Not it. That was wrong. The kitsune was a he. I didn't know *how* I knew, but I'd take it.

"You're beautiful, aren't you," I said, scratching under his chin.

The kitsune rolled over onto his back and put his paws in the air. I took that to mean he wanted belly rubs, and was rewarded with a soft whine once I'd obliged.

A low chuckle escaped from me. I hadn't realised how much I needed something like this. The kitsune didn't need anything from me, other than affection, and here I was giving it to him. He batted one of his paws against my arm, probably to make sure I wouldn't stop with the fuss.

"Attention, please, ladies," the man who seemed to be judging everything called.

As much as I didn't want to, I straightened myself up, leaving the kitsune on the floor at my feet. He popped up almost instantly, and then wound his way around my ankles. I enjoyed his comforting presence. I had no idea what I'd done to make him act like that, especially when one look around the room revealed the other animals had moved away from the women who had been fussing them.

"Thank you for your time this morning. As you know, there are only five tests that make up the competition, and as such, the Prince has decided that we are going to go down to the final ten today."

"Already?" someone muttered.

"Is that not normal?" I whispered to Eliza and Rosemary, certain one of them would know.

Eliza shrugged. "Every Prince does it differently. It isn't unheard of, but most of the time, there's at least three rounds before the final ten are picked."

I had to wonder if this was because Archie knew

about my presence. I searched him out in the crowd, and the moment out gazes locked, a smile lit up his face. Ah. Perhaps it *was* because of me. Perhaps I should feel a little guilty about that, but it was difficult when all I want is to spend the rest of my life with Archie.

"The following ladies are continuing on in the competition," he said.

The room fell silent aside from the calls from the various animals. My kitsune pressed harder against my ankles.

"Lady Rebekah..."

I grimaced. But Eliza had called it. She was still in the running. Hopefully, it was simply because of the political ramifications and not because Archie liked her.

He caught my eye with a brief hand wave. "Sorry," he mouthed.

I nodded ever so slightly, hoping he noticed and took it to mean that I understood why he'd had to do it.

"Lady Eliza..."

The shock on my newest friend's face was evident even while I watched from the corner of my eye.

"Lady Felicia, Lady Helen, Lady Jemma, Lady Rosemary..."

I reached out and squeezed Rosemary's hand, glad she was coming with me on the next part of the competition. I was almost certain she was in love with someone else, which didn't make her competition for Archie's hand.

"Lady Ann, Lady Hazel, Lady Philippa..."

Wait. Was I *not* going to be part of this any more? Had I misunderstood Archie's sorry? Did that actually mean he was sorry I didn't get picked?

"And Lady Cosette."

My eyes fluttered closed and I breathed a sigh of relief. Archie wanted me to be here, I had to remember that.

"The rest of you are to collect your things and make your way back to your homes. We thank you for taking part in this year's competition," the man said.

"No!" one of the women screamed, rushing forward and pushing people out of the way to get to the front. "I won't be dismissed like this. Don't you know who I am?"

I didn't pay any attention to her, instead, my gaze searched for Archie. He looked horrified. As if he hated every moment of this. He likely did. A competition to find him a wife didn't seem in line with any of the other things I knew about him.

"Guards, please," the man said coolly.

Two soldiers entered the stables, taking hold of the woman by each of her elbows and dragging her away. Archie's face echoed the same devastation as I felt myself. And it had nothing to do with the possible embarrassment she was feeling and everything to do with how she'd been treated. I was sure he'd be having words with the organiser after this was done.

Needing some kind of comfort, I crouched down and scratched the top of the kitsune's head.

"I'm sorry I have to leave you," I told him. "If it was up to me, I wouldn't. But that's the way the world works."

He whined, but there was nothing else I could do. No one had said we could take the animals, and as magical creatures, I was sure they were all worth a lot of money. Not the kind of thing to let a nobody like me keep just because I'd formed an attachment to it when we'd met. Even if I had caught the eye of the Prince.

CHAPTER ELEVEN

I CLIMBED THE STAIRS, slowed down by how stuffed I felt after lunch. I didn't think I'd eaten too much, it was just that the food was richer than I was used to, and that meant I felt fuller after eating it.

The corridor to my room was thankfully deserted. I didn't want to run into any of the other women if I didn't have to. They'd want to make small talk and I wasn't in the mood for any of that. We'd been given a free afternoon, though I expected that might change. But for now, I planned to make the most of it by taking the time to have a lie-down. It was far too easy to find myself exhausted by all the things I didn't normally have to do.

I slipped my key into the lock and twisted. It was nice to have a sealed off place of my own. At first, I'd thought the maids would be able to come and go at whim too, but they told me that was only the case for more permanent residents of the castle. A bleak reminder that no one thought I'd be here long.

But they were missing one crucial piece of information. I *knew* Archie. And he liked me. There was no way I was going home.

I might even spend the rest of my life living here.

The door gave way under my weight, and I stepped inside, only to slam it shut again. I didn't lock it behind me, as I didn't want to miss anyone coming and telling me it was time for the next test. If there was one thing I'd learned from being here already, it was that they liked to spring things on us. I slipped the key into my pocket, where it clinked against the one for my tower. I kept moving it from dress to dress, not wanting to leave it behind in case I lost it.

Not that I expected to be able to sneak back into it. Mother would return at some point today, tomorrow at the latest, and she'd discover I wasn't there any longer. Would she search for me? Most people would assume she would. But she hadn't shown me all that much affection over the years, so perhaps she wouldn't care.

I set the book I'd gotten from the library before lunch down on the bed, and leaned back to try and unlace the strings at the back of my dress. The maids didn't seem to understand that I needed to breathe when they did it up. Unable to get the right purchase on them, I gave up and flopped on the bed.

I pulled the book open and flicked to the page I'd marked. A drawing of a kitsune filled the page on the left, and I studied it to try and work out if it was the right kind. I knew next to nothing about the creatures, but after bonding with the one in the stables, I was desperate to learn more about them.

The main difference seemed to be that this one had more tails. Six, to be exact. I scanned the page, trying to find if there was an explanation for it. My gaze caught on a hastily written note.

Kitsune's gain powers as they age, and with each new one, they sprout a new tail. Most are born with two, and have three by the time they are four years of age. The other tails vary in speed. Traits gained by kitsune include things such as camouflage, telekinesis, and teleportation.

Those were useful talents, I had to admit. Though whether they would extend past the kitsune and on to other people was something I had to wonder about.

I drank in the rest of the words on the page, though they didn't tell me very much that I hadn't already guessed or seen in books before this. Kitsunes were real, but rare. I hadn't doubted either of those facts. It had seemed to be the case for all of the creatures in the stable this morning.

A crash sounded from the dresser at the opposite side of the room, and I was on my feet in seconds, wobbling slightly when my skirts got caught around my legs.

"Hello?" My voice shook as I asked. The dresser was nowhere near the door, so it didn't seem likely that it was someone coming to tell me that the next test was about to start. "Who is it?"

A rustling sound pulled my attention to the side of the piece of furniture, and I let out a nervous laugh as I recognised the burnt orange colour of the fur.

I knelt down and held out my hand, making the same noise I had earlier. "I don't think you're supposed to be here," I warned the kitsune. Though a small part of me loved that he'd come to find me despite that.

He trotted forward and pushed his head against my hand, demanding scratches. It only took me a moment to comply. He'd enjoyed it when I'd done that earlier, and I wanted to make him my friend, especially if I was going to be spending a lot more of my life at the palace.

"What's your name?" I asked, despite the fact he didn't seem to be able to talk. Then again, if they could have a lot more tails, then perhaps one of the powers he could develop was the ability to read minds and send telepathic communications.

I waited for a moment in case my theory was right, but nothing came.

"Why don't I call you Fenn?" I suggested.

He pushed harder into my hand in a gesture I was going to take as meaning he liked it.

"Fenn it is, then." I beamed as the kitsune showed me more affection. If Archie thought he was ever getting the creature back, then he had another thing coming. "You're not supposed to be here. You could get us both in trouble." And yet, I couldn't bring myself to regret that. Or to go out of my room and ask someone to go and find me a stable master who could take Fenn back to where he belonged.

After a little while, he became tired of my fussings, and meandered over to the bed. He hopped up with ease, curled up in a ball, and went to sleep. All right then. It seemed my visitor was here for the long run.

Taking my cue from him, I made my way back over to the bed and lay down, pulling the book back towards me. If he was going to stay here, I had to learn as much as I could about kitsune.

I hoped Archie wouldn't be angry about this. I didn't suppose he would be, especially as Fenn had made his way into my room of his own accord. Plus, that wasn't Archie's style either. He was much more likely to have a laid back approach.

But we weren't in the village any more, and I'd do well to remember that. Here, he would be influenced by what his parents, sister, and peers thought. As well as by the reactions of the people around me. If I took *those* factors into account, then I was less certain Fenn would end up staying with me.

I reached out and stroked his soft and silky fur. A small sigh escaped my lips. I hadn't realised how much I wanted unconditional company like this. Even before I'd come to the palace, I'd been a little lonely on the days I couldn't sneak out of the tower. A little companionship from an animal wouldn't have gone amiss.

Fenn lifted his head and studied me with sleepy eyes. Deciding I wasn't a threat, he settled down again and went back to sleep.

Satisfaction thrummed through me. Never mind what Archie, or anyone else, thought of the situation. Fenn trusted me, and that meant the world, even if I couldn't explain why.

My eyes began to droop and the words on my page began to merge as I tried to keep my focus. This wasn't going to happen. I needed to rest, or I'd be no use when the next test came.

I closed the book and pushed it away from me, before resting my head against my arms and letting myself begin to drift off. I hadn't even been trying to sleep for a minute when movement on the bed caught my attention. The next thing I knew, a warm, furry body pressed itself against me, then flopped back down beside me.

Even in my half-asleep state, a smile stretched across my lips. I was the most trusted of the kitsune, and I planned to keep it that way.

With that, the two of us drifted off to sleep, even though it was the middle of the day. This was a luxury I'd never really been able to afford before. Mother would always want me for one task or another.

Before I could contemplate my change in circumstances any more, the darkness of sleep took me, and I drifted off into the peaceful abyss.

CHAPTER TWELVE

"Please tell me you didn't sneak back down to the stables to kidnap him?" Rosemary asked as I stepped out into the gardens to join her so we could make our way to where we'd been instructed to meet.

"You mean Fenn?" I asked, feigning innocence.

"You named him? You're never getting rid of him now," she responded with a light laugh. "You know nothing about kitsune, do you?"

I shook my head. "I found a book in the library, but it didn't tell me very much."

She shrugged, then slipped her arm through mine. "He's imprinted on you. There's no chance you'll ever get away from him now."

"That's all right with me." I paused. "But will the royals let him stay with me? I don't want them to think I came here to steal one of their pets."

The small stones which covered the path crunched under our feet as we made our way down it. A twist in the path led us under a trellis covered in creeping vines and roses. The sweet scent of the flowers permeated the air, reminding us all that summer was beginning.

"It'll be fine. The Prince seems to like you."

My blood turned to ice in my veins. How could she possibly know that? I hadn't told her about knowing Archie, I didn't want her to think I was cheating and report us to someone. Especially as a small part of me constantly wondered if the King would object to me becoming Archie's wife in the end.

"Relax. I only noticed him watching you, I know you haven't done anything against the rules."

"Oh."

We turned another twist in the path, bringing us out onto a larger grass lawn with all the other ladies milling around, chattering away with one another. At only half the number there'd been in the beginning, it seemed a lot emptier than for the previous tests.

"What do you think we're going to be doing?" I asked.

Nerves fluttered in my stomach as I ran through

all of the possible ideas in my head. How could I win the whole competition when I had no idea about the kinds of things that were done at court?

"No idea. Croquet, maybe? Or boules. Those are common enough sports," Rosemary answered.

"And you can play both of them?" I double-checked. If she knew how, then perhaps I stood a chance after all. For whatever reason, Rosemary didn't see me as the competition.

Then again, she hadn't seemed very interested in Archie so far. Just more evidence that she was interested in someone else instead. A small part of me hoped so. But only if it wasn't going to get her in trouble with the rules. The last thing I wanted was for her to end up kicked out of the competition because of it.

"I can," she assured me. "And they're both easy. You'll pick them up in no time."

Fenn yipped from his position between us, and I looked up in time to see Archie striding towards us.

A wide grin spread over my face, one he echoed instantly. At least I didn't have to worry about *him* still being interested.

"I see you've found the missing kitsune, Lady Cosette," he observed.

I giggled, despite an attempt not to. "He made his

way to my room yesterday," I promised. "I don't know why."

Rosemary drifted away to join Eliza and the others, not even saying a word.

"If Lady Rosemary keeps disappearing like that, I'm going to start thinking she doesn't like me," he joked.

Interesting. So he'd come to the same conclusion as I had about Rosemary's feelings. I wondered what it was about him that sent her running, but couldn't come up with any explanations.

"She's lovely," I promised.

"I've no doubt. I'm glad you seem to be making friends here," he observed.

"Yes. Rosemary and Lady Eliza." We'd sat with the other woman at all of our meals after the stables, and she was slowly opening up to us. I found I liked her.

"Good. That'll make choosing the top five easier. Neither of them seem particularly interested in becoming my wife," Archie lamented, though I could tell he wasn't being serious. "I'd be insulted if I didn't already know who I want."

A blush crept to my cheek just as Fenn yipped again.

"Sorry, boy, I didn't mean to ignore you," I said, crouching down and fussing him behind his ears.

Archie followed suit so we were both on the same level as the kitsune. "Oh, sorry, I didn't answer about him."

"That's all right. I'm still learning about him."

"If he went to your room, then it must have been because he felt a connection with you."

"Rosemary said as much."

He chuckled, then reached out and tickled Fenn under the chin. "She's a smart one. It means he sees you as his rightful companion now. As far as I know, there's never been a kitsune who has changed their mind about a connection like this."

My eyes widened and my hand froze in Fenn's silky fur. How had that even happened? All I'd done was follow my instincts when it came to fussing him. I wasn't anything special, and I was certain the kitsune knew that.

"I'm sorry, I didn't mean to steal one of your family pets..."

"You didn't," he assured me. "And even if you did, you'll be family soon anyway. If you still want to, that is."

I reached out with my spare hand and placed it on his knee. "I do," I promised. "But I need to go home after this too, just to set a few things straight."

His eyebrows knitted together, and he wobbled

on his feet. I had to admit, I was struggling to hold the crouched position myself, but Fenn didn't seem anywhere near done demanding fuss.

"What kind of things?" Archie asked.

I opened my mouth to respond, but was cut off by a trumpet and an announcement from the gathered crowd. My eyes narrowed as I located the same man who had been running the rest of the tests about to make an announcement. What terrible timing. I'd much rather stay here with Archie. Or even better, go away with him.

"I have to go." I pointed in the direction of the others.

"You could skip it?" he suggested.

"It's a test, I can't." Though that didn't mean I didn't want to. What would the consequences be if I didn't take part because I was spending time with Archie? Now there was a conundrum.

"It's not a test," he assured me as the two of us rose to our feet.

Fenn pressed himself against my leg, whining for the lack of attention.

"It isn't?"

He shook his head. "It's practice for tomorrow's test. Archery. You can skip it and we can spend some time together..."

I grimaced. "I really want to..."

"But?"

"But I've never done archery before. If I don't go now, how will I pass the test tomorrow? If I want to win, then I need to prove to people who aren't you that I'm worthy," I pointed out.

"Ah. That is problematic. Perhaps I should stay and help, then?"

My heart skipped a beat at the thought of that. I loved the idea of spending more time with him, even if I had to learn a new skill to take advantage of it.

"Well, I could use a tutor."

The corner of his lips cracked up into a smirk. "Shall we, then?"

He held out his arm, and I slipped my own through it, resting my hand on it the way we had many times in the village. Somehow, it felt different here. Probably because there were so many people watching at every turn.

The two of us walked our way over to the archery range, where the other women had paired off and were beginning to practice. The twang of the bowstring being released, and the whistles of arrows flying through the air was enough to fill me with a sense of dread. How was I going to compete with seasoned bow-women tomorrow?

"Relax," Archie instructed. "You're going to be fine."

"That's easy for you to say, you've been doing this since you were five," I muttered.

"Seven, actually," he joked. "Mother was very clear on that. She didn't want me accidentally hurting myself, or something like that."

"You're not filling me with much hope."

Archie didn't listen to my refusals, and pressed a bow into my hands.

"You're going to want to tell your kitsune not to interfere."

"Fenn," I corrected. "That's his name."

He nodded.

"Will he really do something about it?"

"I don't know," he admitted. "But telekinesis is part of the kitsune repertoire, and if he's already as attached to you as he seems, then he'll want to help you in all the ways he can, even if he shouldn't."

Taking his suggestion to heart, I crouched down again, resting my bow across my legs and looking into the cutest face I'd ever seen in my life. How had I lived this long without finding a creature like this?

"Fenn, I need you to behave," I said carefully, hoping I was using the right words. "I need to do this without you."

He sat on his haunches and cocked his head to the side, as if questioning me.

"Please?"

He dipped his snout.

Hmm. Had he understood me? Or was I trying to read too much into it?

"Thank you," I said for good measure, before returning to my upright state. "Now what?" I asked Archie.

He guided me through the motions, setting my posture right, and correcting how I was holding the arrow. Apparently, I'd been doing something wrong when it came to the flight? I wasn't sure. None of the words were familiar, and it was becoming more and more difficult to concentrate.

"Now try shooting," Archie instructed, stepping back to give me some space.

Rebekah glared at me from over his shoulder. I hadn't paid much attention to her while Archie had been helping me, but now I could see her face, the malcontent was impossible to ignore. The moment his back was turned, I knew I should be scared for my life. She was here to win. But not for the same reasons I was. She didn't care about the man behind the crown, that much was becoming ever clearer from the things she said.

I took a deep breath and notched an arrow. Following Archie's instructions, I pulled it back and lined it up with the target in front of me. I could do this. He'd taught me how, and now I was going to prove I was a quick learner.

With nothing else for it, I let go of the bowstring. The sound reverberated in my ear, louder than it had sounded while other people had done it.

I was so distracted, I hardly noticed my arrow hitting the target. Though only in the outside circle. I wasn't completely sure what that meant, but it wasn't the best marks.

"It's a shame you can't hit the bullseye, Miss Cosette," Rebekah said snidely.

"Everyone was a beginner at one stage or other, Lady Rebekah," Archie answered coolly.

There was no love lost between the two of them, then. I tried to push away the smugness that rose within me at the realisation.

"If I remember correctly, you couldn't even hit the target the first time you entered the range," one of the other women said. Phillipa. I had to be better at remembering my competitors' names.

A scowl stole over Rebekah's face. "Well, if I had the same favouritism as Miss Cosette is getting, then I'd have hit first time too. She has a new pet too. Obviously the royal family doesn't need the likes of me and Father any more." Bitterness dripped from every word.

"I'm sure he was just helping Cosette because she

needed it," Eliza said softly, no doubt trying to calm the rising tensions. She would be a good ally to have in the future as well as now. I should remember that for once this is all over.

Rebekah's sarcastic laugh filled the surrounding area, sending a shiver down my spine. "What do you know? You're just as bad cosying up to the *Silvers*." Her disdain cut through me like a knife.

I had to ignore her. I knew how Archie felt, and I had Fenn by my side. This was all being caused because she was jealous, no other reason.

"I'm sorry, Cosette, but she's right that I need to talk to the others," Archie whispered to me.

"I understand." Even if it hurt to think of him standing so close to the other women. I knew saying anything about it would only look bad on me.

"I wish I was spending more of my time with you," he promised. "But keep practising. You'll be a good markswoman before you know it."

I tried to give him a reassuring smile, but I didn't think I managed. Despite that, he went off to talk with some of the other ladies.

It wasn't his fault. I needed to remember that and get a hold on my jealousy. He was the centre of this competition, he had to act like it was a fair race right up until the end.

"Don't worry about Rebekah," Eliza said from

right beside me. I'd been so consumed with my thoughts I hadn't heard her approach.

"Easier said than done," I muttered.

She gave me a conspiratorial smile. "She's just jealous. None of us are blind. We can see the way the Prince is looking at you. She hates it, because she knows she doesn't have half of your personality. And you have a kitsune on top of that. You're winning the lottery in her eyes."

"I suppose I am," I admitted. "But aren't the others jealous too? And you..."

"The Prince is lovely," she said. "But he isn't my type. The others...I don't think you'll have any problems. They all know what the competition is. Rebekah's problem is that she expected to win it, and is only now realising she can't guarantee that. She'll get over it."

"I hope you're right." And hopefully, I'd get better at dealing with the woman.

"I'm sorry, I'm keeping you from your practice. Let me know if you need help. I'm not the best at this, but I've been learning for years, so I should be able to give a few pointers," Eliza promised.

"Thank you, I appreciate it." And not only because she'd admitted to not being interested in Archie.

She smiled, then headed back to her station to pick up her own bow.

Right. Practice. It was the last thing I wanted to do, but right now, I had no choice in the matter. If I wanted to pass tomorrow's test, then I was going to have to try and master this.

And quickly.

CHAPTER THIRTEEN

How was I going to manage this? Even with spending most of yesterday practising, there was no way I could beat the women who'd been shooting for most of their lives. I supposed that, technically, I only had to beat five of them, but that didn't really mean anything. I still wouldn't be able to.

Fenn seemed to sense my discomfort, and pressed himself more tightly against my leg. It made walking a little more difficult, but I appreciated his presence more than he could ever know. It was nice having a companion at all times. Not being alone was good.

But it didn't solve the problem on hand. My best bet was to hope the whole thing was rigged anyway. Archie had mentioned choosing the top five, so I could cling to that being the truth. Perhaps if I managed to get a passable score, that would be all it took.

I wasn't naive enough to think it would work like that. The competition was hardly about Archie at all, though I hadn't had enough alone time to confirm it with him. The whole point of this was to show to the court that the woman who became Queen was suited to the task, though personally I didn't see what some of the tasks had to do with that.

"No doing anything funny," I warned Fenn. "Win or lose, I have to do it on my own merit."

He looked up at me and cocked his head to the side.

"I'm serious," I warned.

He skipped out ahead of me and ran a little circle before returning to his original spot. I had no idea what it meant, but I suspected I'd be able to work it out in time. I simply needed to get to know him better. Two days was hardly enough time to properly get to know an animal, even if it was one who had barely left my side in that entire time.

The other ladies were all standing in front of their targets. Was I late? I didn't think so. To be sure, I hurried over to the final one. I didn't know if it had been left empty on purpose, but I couldn't help noticing that it was the one closest to the royal box. Was that a good thing, or not? On the one hand, I'd be closer to Archie, which meant more moral support. On the other, his parents and the rest of the court would see just how badly I did first hand. There wouldn't be any hiding at all.

I picked up the bow and weighed it in my hands. Something about it felt off. Not like the one I'd used yesterday, but I wasn't sure why.

Never mind. It was probably just a different one and I'd be used to it after an arrow or two.

"Good morning, ladies," the announcer said.

Had he ever told us his name? It felt odd that I didn't know it, though I didn't need to in order to pay attention to him. Perhaps that was why he didn't tell anyone about it. More likely, he'd been around the court for years, and everyone already knew his name. It was just because I was a new addition that I was behind.

"As you are aware, today you'll be participating in a competition within the competition..."

Laughter ran through the assembled courtiers, though none of the women waiting with me laughed. At least I wasn't the only one who was nervous. That was a little reassuring. Though not much. If they felt that way and could shoot, then I was doomed.

No. I wasn't going to let myself think like that. I could do this, because I had to do it.

And not just because I didn't want to see the smug look on Rebekah's face when I lost. She wouldn't let me live it down, ever. And she was likely to still be at court once all of this was over too.

"You will all be shooting at the same time," the man announced. "Assessors will be walking behind you in order to award marks for how you perform."

Relief flooded through me at that. It wasn't as good as not having to shoot at all, but it was better than having to fail while everyone was watching just me. So long as I didn't do anything noteworthy, then most people probably wouldn't even glance my way. They'd want to watch the people who they considered to be the real contenders.

Rebekah and Felicia, from what I'd heard. Both of whom would have no problem with a challenge such as this one.

"You may begin."

Everyone lurched into motion, notching arrows and letting them sail towards the targets within moments. I almost did the same, not wanting to be left behind. But that wasn't the best way to deal with this situation. I didn't have the same skills as they did, so instead, I'd make each of my arrows count and try my best.

I took a couple of deep breaths, then pulled an arrow out of the quiver left out for me.

It wasn't until I was about to notch it that I noticed the feathering was wrong. Almost as if it had gotten damaged or wet. I set the arrow down and pulled out each of the others in turn. All of them had the same problem.

I frowned. What should I do about that? Had Rebekah done this in order to make things worse for me? I wouldn't have put it past her, but with no proof, there wasn't any point in making a scene.

Instead, I gestured for one of the staff to make their way over to me.

"Is everything all right, Lady Cosette?" the woman asked, looking between me and the arrows in my hand with interest.

"I think there's been some damage to the fletching," I said, hoping what I thought I was seeing was actually the case. There'd be nothing more embarrassing than being told I'd made a mistake right now. "Would it be possible to get a fresh quiver?"

"Of course, my Lady. Those don't look right to me. I'll go fetch you another one."

"Thank you, I appreciate it."

She was back within a couple of minutes with a fresh one over her shoulder. She shrugged it off, then held it out to me. "Would you like to check the arrows before I set it down?"

"Yes, please." I took the first one out and examined it. Then the second, and the third. I should have gone to the library to find a book that might help. But it was too late to wish that now. All I could do was trust my instincts, and those said that these arrows were good. "Thank you," I said to the woman.

"You're welcome, my lady." She dipped her head, then set down the quiver.

With nothing else for it, I notched the first arrow and prepared to let it sail towards the target. I hoped the delay in getting started wouldn't count against me. But perhaps that had been Rebekah's ploy the entire time. No doubt she'd done something to some of the other ladies' arrows too, but I wasn't about to accuse her of anything. Nothing could make me foolish enough to do that, especially when I knew she had no claim over Archie's heart.

I carried on shooting. My arrows hit the target each time, which amazed me, but they didn't get particularly good scores. I had no idea how I was going to come out in the top five at this rate. There was no way that half of the assembled women would mess up as badly as I was.

A sharp snap sounded, and I whipped my head around, breaking the pact I had with myself not to look at what the others were doing.

Phillipa stood there with her bow in hand, the string dangling to the floor where an arrow lay. I assumed that had been notched up until a moment ago.

I was about to step forward and ask if she was all right, but the pure hatred in her eyes stopped me in my tracks.

"How *dare* you?" she seethed, turning and marching straight over to Rebekah.

Well, at least I knew I was right. Though perhaps not, given the surprise on my rival's face.

"You couldn't stand the idea of anyone else potentially winning this thing, could you?" Phillipa screeched.

"Were you the one who greased my bow too?" Hazel demanded too.

I exchanged a worried glance with Eliza, who had ended up at the target next to mine. What would be the best thing for us to do now? Should we go back to shooting and pretend none of this was happening? We'd been told that decorum and how we acted could get us kicked out at any point, did that include this?

"That concludes this morning's tournament," the announcer said.

I guessed that answered that one. I calmly set my bow down next to my quiver and made my way over to where he was standing along with the other girls. I wanted to ask Eliza and Rosemary about what had just happened, but this didn't seem like the best time to do that.

Rebekah was almost green with worry as she approached. Huh. Had I been wrong? Was she innocent of the sabotage after all?

"As you may have guessed, there is now to be an elimination. As per the Prince's request, we are announcing the final five. For the archery tournament, you have not been ranked based on your scores, but on how you dealt with issues which arose during the course of the competition."

I sighed with relief. I'd kept a level head. That more than made up for the terrible marks. I hoped. Perhaps this rule had been brought in simply so there was an excuse to keep me.

Fenn pushed against my leg, and I leaned it back into him, appreciating the comfort he was offering. I should have asked Mother for a pet years ago.

I pushed aside the twinge of guilt at the thought of Mother. Things were complicated with her to say the least. Hopefully, once this was over, Archie could help me find her and then...well, I wasn't sure what then. But I needed some closure when it came to Mother.

"The following competitors are advancing to the next round. Lady Cosette, Lady Eliza, and Lady Rosemary..."

Even though I'd expected all three of our names after what Archie said to me, relief still flooded through me as I realised we'd all be part of the next phase. And only some of it came from knowing neither of my friends were interested in him. Though it did raise the question of *who* had caught their eyes.

"Both of the Silvers?" Rebekah muttered from behind me, disbelief in her voice.

The childish part of me wanted to turn around and stick my tongue out at her. But that kind of behaviour would likely get me kicked out.

"Lady Felicia..."

Also not a surprise. Though I wished Archie's childhood sweetheart hadn't still been in the race. But she was the perfect candidate. Serene, elegant, and soft-spoken. She'd have made a good queen in other circumstances.

"And Lady Rebekah."

What?

No.

Surely not.

She might not have sabotaged everyone today, but she probably thought about it, despite the fact she shouldn't have. I wouldn't put anything past the woman.

"Thank you for your attendance today. If you are

one of the five ladies whose name has been called, you will shortly each be having a date with the Prince. For the five ladies who have not been called, I have to apologise, but you must leave the competition and return to your homes."

Hazel spun on her heels and pushed through us, not caring who she knocked to the side. Phillipa had a very different approach, and did nothing more than stand and glare at Rebekah.

At least they weren't focusing their hatred on me. It was a selfish thought, but one I needed to focus on in order to preserve my own sanity.

It was only after they'd left that the rest of what the announcer had said sank in. We were going to have alone time with Archie.

Though I suspected mine would be interrupted by an over-friendly kitsune, whether I liked it or not.

CHAPTER FOURTEEN

Archie guided me into a part of the gardens I hadn't visited before. Not that it meant much that I hadn't. Everything was happening so quickly that I hadn't had time to explore much. In fact, I was exhausted from simply being around so many people. I wasn't used to it.

Fenn ran around us, travelling a little further away from me now that it was only the two of us and him. It seemed I wasn't the only one who didn't like being around too many people.

"It isn't the same as the waterfall, but when I was trying to think of the best place to take you, this was what sprang to mind," he said as he drew me through a trellis with a hand on the small of my back.

I gasped as I took in the stunning lake in front of us. The water sparkled in the midday sun, and I was almost certain I could see fish swimming about in it even from here.

"It's beautiful," I admitted. "Thank you."

"You're welcome. I hope you're hungry though, the cooks packed us a small feast."

I chuckled. "Maybe they thought the others would be with us too?" I was fishing for information, something he'd probably guess. But it didn't matter. I hated the idea of him spending one-on-one time with the others, even though I knew two of them weren't interested in him.

"I doubt it. They're busy preparing the outrageously formal candlelit dinner I was going to do for Rebekah." He grimaced as he said her name. "Do you think it would be enough for her?"

"Nothing short of a coronation would be," I muttered.

Archie's laugh bellowed around me. "I think you might be onto something there. Doesn't she realise that by acting that way, she makes it so she's *less* likely to get what she wants?"

I shrugged. "Some people are like that."

I sat on the picnic blanket, leaning back and letting the heat from the sun warm me.

"I can't work out what to do with your friends, though," he admitted. "I want them to have a good time, but there's no use pretending at anything if they're not interested in me." He joined me on the picnic blanket and started unpacking the food.

Within seconds, it was clear how different this picnic would be from our last one. Nothing he'd brought was simple. And the variety was astounding. I was glad we were still so close to the kitchens considering how much we were going to end up not eating.

"You could ask them?" I offered. "Neither of them would be funny about it."

"That's a good idea, thank you." He poured some wine into two goblets, then handed one to me.

"What about Felicia?" I asked.

Perhaps I shouldn't. It was already bad enough hearing about the dates he was going to go on with the girls he didn't have a history with. But Felicia had been his childhood sweetheart. There had to still be some residuals of that left, whether the two of them liked it or not.

He sighed loudly. "I'm stuck there too. My relationship with Felicia is complicated at best."

"How come?" I took a sip of wine while I waited for him to elaborate. I needed to be careful I didn't drink too much.

He glanced around, checking we were alone. There were some guards at the entrances to the gardens, but no one else. And they weren't a particular risk given they were probably paid to be silent about what they overheard.

"Felicia was too old for my sister and her friends, but desperately wanted to be around them. After a while, it became so painful to watch her trying to fit in, that *I* started doing it so she wouldn't feel bad. I hate to say as a lesson in diplomacy, but that's what it was. In my youthful ignorance, I thought I was helping a subject of mine who was in pain. She took it as romantic interest, and one thing led to another. I regret it now, because it wasn't fair to either of us. But at the time, there was nothing I could do about that."

I simply nodded as I pulled a leg of chicken into pieces and threw them in Fenn's direction. He jumped up and caught each one as it reached him.

"I have to ask you something," I said.

"About Felicia?" He took a drink.

"No. I understand that." And was actually relieved after hearing what he had to say. It was good to know that the feelings were one-sided, even if that would hurt her in the end. "It's about after all of this."

"You mean after you agree to become my queen?" he countered.

I chuckled. "Yes. After that."

"What is it?"

I set the chicken bone down and met his gaze.

"After the competition is over. I need you to take me home."

His face fell.

I reached out and took his hand in mine. "Not forever. Just for a day. Maybe even a couple of hours. I have no idea how far away the village is," I admitted.

He cocked his head to the side, studying me intently. "You don't?"

"No. I was kidnapped from the path between the village and the tower..." The moment I started talking about it, I found everything falling out. Confusion and anger warred in his eyes as I told him about the holding cells, then awe over the silver blood, and relief when I got to the part where I was in the palace and planning to look for him during the ball.

It was actually crazy how much had happened.

Fenn seemed to have decided we'd ignored him enough, and stuck his nose into the picnic basket to try and find more food. I left him to it.

"Why did you always go back to the tower? You never seemed to like it much," he asked.

"Mother was there. She was all I'd ever known, and it was hard to let go of that. Even if she did keep me locked up."

"I wonder why she did that," he mused.

It was hard not to laugh at that question. Why *had* Mother kept me away from the world? It was a question I'd been trying to find the answer to for longer than I cared to think about, especially as I didn't *have* any possible answers.

"I don't know," I admitted. "In the past week, I've wondered if it was something to do with my silver blood. It's worth something, right? To people who can make potions and magical trinkets and stuff?"

He nodded. "I suppose that's as reasonable an explanation as any. But why do you want to go back?" he asked.

"Because I need to know. I want her to tell me why she kept me locked up. I think it will give me some closure on that part of my life."

He nodded. "I can understand that. If I hadn't found you at the ball, then I'd have gone back to the village to wait for you, even if it was just for an explanation as to why you didn't want to come with me."

I reached out and took his hand in mine, giving it a squeeze. "All I thought about was getting back to you," I promised.

"I know."

He leaned in, and I did the same, hoping we'd be able to kiss for the first time in days. It had been strange seeing him so often, yet not feeling like we could fully be ourselves.

Fenn barked, pulling the two of us out of our trance. I reached out to pet him, hoping it would calm whatever was going on with him.

My eyes widened as I recognised the woman walking through the nearest trellis. She stopped in her tracks and pressed a hand over her heart. There was something off about her reaction to the two of us, but I wasn't sure what it was.

"Oh, I'm so sorry, I didn't realise the two of you were here. Please forgive me, Lady Cosette, Archibald." Felicia dipped her head at each of us in turn.

"It's not a problem, Lady Felicia," Archie responded, stiffening slightly.

Was it the disappointment in not being able to kiss? Or was it the knowledge that she'd caught us.

"I'll find somewhere else to walk."

Before we could say anything else, she'd disappeared back the way she came.

I frowned, trying to work out what had just happened, and why.

"I hope she's all right," I said eventually.

"She will be," he promised. "But that's enough talk of serious things. Why don't we paddle in the lake?"

"Paddle?" I echoed. "I'd never manage to get this dress off by myself. I doubt you could either."

He chuckled. "I'll admit, I've never tried. But it wouldn't be proper either. We have to wait until after the wedding for things like that."

"How boring."

"It is rather. But for now, we can paddle."

"Very well." I lifted my dress up far further than I should if the maids were to be believed. I stripped off the socks and garters I was wearing, having already kicked off my shoes once we'd sat down. "I'm as ready as I'll ever be," I admitted.

"Me too," Archie responded, jumping to his feet. The bottom of his breaches were rolled up to leave his feet and ankles bare.

It looked as if we weren't going very far into the lake. I was sure we'd be able to change that at a later date.

Fenn perked up as he realised we were about to move. And, to my surprise, he followed the two of us to the water's edge.

I dipped my toe in and squealed. "It's cold."

"Of course it is, the day's not that old yet," Archie teased, before jumping straight in.

The water splashed up around us, drenching part of my dress, along with Fenn.

The kitsune wasn't put off, though, as he jumped in, following Archie's lead.

With nothing left to lose, and only a small amount of guilt for the extra work this would cause the maids, I jumped in with the two of them, but didn't make as much of a splash, much to my disappointment.

Small fish darted around our feet, and I leaned down to try and catch one, mostly just to see if I could. I'd let it go straight after.

I stumbled forward, almost losing my balance, only to be saved by Archie grabbing hold of my arms.

"Are you all right?" he asked as he helped me stand back up.

The two of us were so close I could feel the heat of his body radiating against me.

"Better than I have been all week," I whispered, my gaze flicking down to his lips. It had been too long since I'd kissed him, and I didn't plan on waiting any longer.

He raised one of his hands and stroked a stray strand of hair away from my face. I stepped even closer to him. The moment our lips touched, every care and worry I'd had over the past week slipped away. He held me tight, and we said all the things we hadn't and couldn't.

If there had been any doubts in my mind about whether I wanted to be his wife, and there weren't, then this kiss was all I needed in order to chase them away.

Archie was going to be my life for as long as the two of us lived. And I couldn't wait to start.

CHAPTER FIFTEEN

I WAVED goodbye to Rosemary as she slipped back into her room, and turned to my own. I hadn't eaten much at dinner, since I'd still been full from the picnic lunch with Archie. We'd taken a long time to eat the food he'd brought with him, thought I suspected that was mostly because we knew the longer it took us, the more time we'd get to spend together. And that was important to us.

Fenn jumped up and down beside me as I unlocked the door, no doubt eager to climb onto the bed and go to sleep. That seemed to be one of his favourite places to rest.

"All right, nearly there." I pushed the door open, and he darted in.

It only took him a moment to start growling. I

paused, unsure whether I should go in and soothe him, or call for the guards to check the room first.

A yelp from inside decided me, and I pushed open the door, ready to take on whoever was hurting my kitsune. I wasn't sure *what* I would do, but it would definitely be something.

I froze in my tracks the moment I was in the room.

"Mother?"

There wasn't much doubt that it was her standing there, a scowl on her face which could have stopped even the King from doing what he was supposed to.

With great difficulty, I pulled my gaze away from her and scanned the room for Fenn. I relaxed as soon as I spotted his eyes sparkling from under the bed. If he was there, then no one could hurt him.

"What are you doing here?" I asked, folding my arms across my chest and waiting for an explanation. How had she even found out where I was? Considering *I'd* had no idea where I was going or why, she shouldn't be here yet. Or at all.

"I could ask you the same thing." She raised an eyebrow.

"I was kidnapped."

"And brought to the palace? You're bad at lying, you shouldn't bother trying, Cosette."

"I'm not lying," I countered. "I was taken from the path to the tower and taken to a cell. Then to here." If she didn't believe me, then that was her problem. It *was* the truth.

"You were outside the tower?" She began to pace the room.

I moved instinctively, keeping as much distance between the two of us as I could. It was only when she was in front of the door, and my only escape route, that I realised what she'd done.

"Yes. I was outside the tower." There was no point pretending otherwise. If things did come out further down the line, then the last thing I wanted was to be caught in a lie.

"What were you doing outside?" she seethed.

"Exploring the village." *Falling in love*. Not that I was going to say the last part out loud. It would only give her something to use against me.

"You're lucky someone worked out who you were and came to find me."

"Someone in the palace?" There were only two people who knew where I'd come from. Archie, and the guard who'd come with me. But he'd disappeared days ago, and I wasn't convinced he knew enough about what was going on to report to Mother.

Did that mean Archie had done it?

No. He'd seemed surprised when I mentioned it

earlier. Though perhaps he'd done this as a bit of a surprise? If so, then it was about to backfire on him.

"It's time to come home, Cosette."

"No," I blurted.

She didn't hide her shock very well. Then again, even I was surprised by the firmness of my refusal. "No?"

"I have to stay."

"No. You don't. You're coming home, and then you're going to tell me exactly how you escaped from the tower so I can make sure it doesn't happen again," she insists.

"No, Mother. I'm not coming back. I have the competition to win..."

She cackled. "Competition? To win the Prince's hand in marriage? You're never going to win that."

"Then why did one of the other ladies tell you where I was to get me out of the way?" I asked, hoping I was right and that it wasn't Archie who had turned me in.

A brief shot of surprise flickered through her eyes.

Ah-ha. So I *was* right. Rebekah seemed the most likely culprit, but I supposed I didn't know any of the others well enough to judge. Though I doubted it was either of my new friends. Neither Eliza nor Rosemary seemed to have much interest in Archie.

"None of that matters. You're a peasant. You're not the kind of woman anyone wants to be Queen."

"Other than the Prince," I pointed out. "And I'm pretty sure his opinion is the one that matters the most."

Mother sighed dramatically and stepped forward.

I moved backwards in response, wanting to keep one step ahead of her if possible. At least, that was the theory until my back hit the wall. So much for that.

I eyed her up and down, wondering if I could outrun her. It seemed unlikely. I glanced down at Fenn, who was still hiding under the bed. I wished I knew how kitsune worked, and if there was any way for him to help. But without being sure, I wasn't going to put him in danger. That would be beyond cruel.

"I was going to come talk to you after the competition was over," I said weakly. I still hadn't decided what I would have said to her, but I supposed none of that mattered any more."

"After is too late, Cosette." She pulled something out of her pocket and threw it in my face.

"Arc-" I coughed, cutting off my cry for the one person I knew had the power to help.

Whatever it was she'd thrown at me tickled the

back of my throat, making it feel far drier than it should. What had she done to me? It wasn't right.

I gasped and doubled over, trying to ignore the sick feeling in my stomach. My knees buckled, and I ended up on the ground. I hoped I wasn't going to ruin the dress the maids had made for me. They worked hard to make it beautiful.

My vision began to swim, but I reached out for Fenn all the same. "Archie," I whispered, hoping the kitsune would understand that I wanted him to go get help.

As my world went dark, I tried to hold on to the knowledge that Archie knew roughly where my tower was. I wouldn't be held against my will for too long.

I hoped.

CHAPTER SIXTEEN

I GROANED and reached up to rub my head. What had I done to deserve waking up like this? I searched my memory, but nothing came to me. The hard floorboards were making my back ache. Why hadn't I made it to the bed? Shouldn't I be curled up with Fenn? Even if I'd done something stupid, I didn't imagine I wouldn't have ended up back there.

Oh.

Wait.

Mother.

That's what had happened. She'd found me after being tipped off by one of the other women in the competition. Well, either Rebekah or Felicia. Neither of my friends made sense.

My eyes snapped open, and I sat up. My head began to spin, but other than taking things a little bit slower, there was nothing I could do about it other than grin and bear the sensation.

Slowly, I climbed to my feet and did a visual check on myself. I was still wearing the same green gown I'd worn to dinner. My shoes were still on the right feet too. The only difference was my long hair felt like it was coming out of its braid, and there was a heavy bandage on my right arm. I wondered where that had come from. No doubt it was Mother trying to control me in some way.

I didn't even have to look around me to know that I was back in the tower. But that wasn't necessarily a bad thing. I knew how to get out. And I wasn't going to waste time trying it. I had no idea how to get back to the palace from here, but I could think of a few places where Archie would try and find me, which would give me a chance.

There was no point wasting another moment in here. Especially when I didn't know where Mother had gone to. She often disappeared for the day, but that didn't mean she was already gone. She could be in her workroom, or downstairs. And no matter what happened, I had to be careful.

I made my way out of the room and onto the landing at the top of the stairs. And then couldn't get any further.

What I could only describe as a fence stretched

up in front of me, blocking my way down to the kitchen and downstairs.

And my way out.

She'd thought of a way to stop me even without knowing *how* I'd gotten out. Though it wouldn't take a genius to work out how when there were no signs of my escape.

"Mother?" I called, then listened intently for any sign that she was there but not responding. I'd been on my own in the tower often enough over the years to know how it sounded when it was empty.

Certain she wasn't around, I grasped two of the bars and began to shake. For a moment, the cool metal burned my bare skin, but the sensation was over so quickly that I assumed it had been in my mind. It was simply because the metal was cold.

And unfortunately, not budging.

I let go and stepped back. How could I get it out of my way with the tools I had in my bedroom? Which were slim to none. And I imagined even less now. Mother wasn't a fool, she wouldn't have left me anything that could get past her barrier. And I hated her for it.

But wait. Her secret room was on this side of the fence. Perhaps there was something in there I could use. No matter how cautious she was being, I was certain she wouldn't have thought to empty *that* room.

I paused in front of the door, trying to get past years of knowing I wasn't supposed to go in. Could I really do this?

I cleared my thoughts with a shake of my head. I had to do this if I wanted to escape. And it was clear I couldn't stay here. Not if Mother was going to force me. I needed to get back to the palace. Back to Archie, and Fenn. They were what my life consisted of right now. Perhaps in time, I could rebuild my relationship with Mother. She was my only family, and I didn't actually want to lose her for good.

With a deep breath in to steady my nerves, I pushed the door open. At first, it didn't budge, seemingly too stiff to move from just my light frame's pressure. But then, it swung open, revealing the contents within.

Things whistled, popped, and glimmered, making it almost impossible to work out what was going on at first. But then it all started to slot into place. The room was being used for some kind of science or potion making.

Silver blood. Good for potion making and magical items.

No. She couldn't have been. Could she? Was that why she kept me locked up in the tower not so long?

And when she went out for her monthly jaunts, was it simply so she could sell the things she made from my blood?

One thing was for certain, I needed to be more certain that's what this was. As much as I didn't want to, I took a step into the room and started scanning the shelves for anything more concrete.

There were a lot of gadgets and gizmos that I wasn't able to put a name to. Some of them looked sharp, others like they would be able to help drain blood.

When had she been doing it to me? In my sleep? Or had she been using something on me like they did in my room at the palace? The mere idea of that sent a shiver down my spine. How could my own Mother do something like that to me? What had I done to deserve it?

A small bottle caught my attention. I reached out and closed my fingers around it. I opened my hand and stared down at it, unsure how to process the words inscribed on the bottle's label.

Silver Blood, Young Woman, Eighteen.

Seeing it left very little doubt about what Mother was doing. And why she'd kept me here. My heart broke as I considered all the years of being left alone and barely being acknowledged. I'd missed out on so much, and for what? So Mother could drain my blood and sell it? Why hadn't she just asked? I'd have been confused, but I wouldn't have denied her despite her coldness towards me.

What was she even doing with the money? It certainly didn't seem as if we used it to live off, given how little upkeep the tower actually had. Though perhaps she spent it when she was gone on her little trips.

I suspected I'd never know. It wasn't like she'd be honest with me, even if I gave her the chance to be.

All of this simply meant that it was definitely time for me to get out of the tower. I'd climb down the outside wall if I had to. Though that probably wasn't the most practical solution.

"Cosette?" Mother's voice called from the lower room.

Panic filled me. What was I going to do now?

With nothing else for it, I shoved the bottle of blood in my pocket, the glass clinking against the two keys I had in there. I was surprised Mother hadn't searched me when we'd arrived back here.

But that didn't matter. Right now, I needed to get back to my room and pretend to be knocked out still. That way, I'd have time to plot my escape.

Hopefully.

I rushed back into my room only to find the last thing I expected waiting for me on the bed.

"Fenn?" I cocked my head to the side, and the Kitsune did the same. "What are you doing here?"

He got up on all fours and turned around, swinging his tails at me.

His *four* tails.

"Did you gain another power?" I whispered hastily.

He cocked his head to the side and gave a small yip. I was going to take that as a yes.

"Was it teleportation?"

He made the same gesture. Definitely a yes, then. Otherwise, I had no idea how he'd gotten here.

"Cosette?" Mother called again.

The sounds of her starting to climb the stairs reached my ears. Thankfully, the gate she'd installed should slow her down. I had to hope it would give me enough time for the next bit.

"Can you take me back to the palace?" I whispered.

He yipped again. Relief flooded through me.

"We have to go fast," I warned him as a metal on metal sound reached my ears. Mother was going to be here any moment.

Fenn moved closer to me, pressing his body against mine.

Not wanting to take any risks, I wrapped myself

tightly around him and held on. "Take me to Rosemary's room, please," I whispered.

Air rushed past my ears and the whole world began to spin, but it didn't scare me. This was my only way out. And I knew Fenn would never hurt me.

CHAPTER SEVENTEEN

I CRASHED to the floor with a thump, Fenn collapsed next to me in a heap. The journey had taken a lot out of him. I'd have to make sure I didn't ask him to do something like this very often, he wouldn't be able to cope.

I propped myself up and looked around, only to find Rosemary and Eliza looking like they'd just sprung apart, complete with matching guilty expressions.

Ah. The pieces slotted into place. This was why the pair of them didn't seem interested in Archie. They had feelings for one another.

"Cosette, what happened?" Rosemary asked, seeming to snap back to attention after my random appearance.

"Fenn learned to teleport," I muttered.

"And he brought you here?" Eliza asked, straightening out her skirts so she appeared less flustered. She was better at this than Rosemary was.

"I asked him to," I admitted. "Well, I asked him to bring me to Rosemary's room. My Mother kidnapped me from mine. I think she was tipped off that I was here by one of the others. Probably Rebekah, she's had it out for me since I arrived."

Eliza shook her head. "Not Rebekah, Felicia."

"Really?" My eyebrows knitted together.

I pushed myself off the floor while I waited for one of them to respond.

"I heard her talking to someone about it," Eliza admitted. "I actually came to warn you, but when I got to your room, no one was there. So I stopped by Rosemary's to see if she'd seen you." She tucked a strand of hair behind her ear.

"Ah. I see. I suppose that makes sense. Rebekah doesn't think she needs to sabotage me in order to win," I mused.

Rosemary nodded in agreement. "Exactly. But then, what do we do about it? And how do we explain how you got back from the tower?"

"That bit's easy," I pointed out as I scooped poor exhausted Fenn up into my arms. I wished he hadn't had to do such a long teleport for his first go. "And we'll just tell Archie about the rest. So long as you're all right with vouching for me, Eliza?"

"Of course I will," she said hastily, glancing at Rosemary.

"I won't tell anyone what I burst in on regardless of if you help me or not," I promised. "Your secret is safe with me for as long as the two of you want it to be a secret."

They exchanged a knowing look, as if they were communicating without saying words. Just how far had a relationship gone between the two of them?

"Are you sure?" Rosemary whispered. "You could outright win if you told the Prince."

I shook my head. "It's not my secret to tell. Besides, I don't *need* to cheat to win Archie's heart."

"Wait, why do you keep calling him Archie? Do you mean the Prince?" Eliza's eyes were as wide as they could possibly go. Clearly I wasn't the only one who'd worked out some relationship secrets.

"Oh, sorry. Yes. I've known Archie for a long time. He actually asked me to marry him before all of this started. Then I got kidnapped, brought here, then reunited with him without realising it...none of it was planned, I promise."

Rosemary burst into fits of laughter. "Are you trying to tell me that all this time, Rebekah has been preening around thinking she's going to win by default, but the Prince has been engaged to you?"

Even Eliza chuckled at the description.

"I wouldn't put it that way," I murmured. "But since we saw each other at the ball it's been fairly certain. But I had to win for the other people at court to take me seriously."

"How did you meet?" Eliza asked, becoming more and more animated the longer we spent on subjects that weren't her. "Have you kissed? When are you getting married? What do you want your wedding dress to look like?"

Fenn wriggled in my arms, clearly recovered from his exhaustion. I let him jump down.

"I'll answer all your questions and more, I promise. But first, we need to find Archie and tell him about what's happening. I need some protection from Mother, I don't imagine she'll be happy when she discovers I'm gone."

And it wasn't like I had a head start. The only potential advantage was that she had no idea *how* I'd left, or where I'd gone. Perhaps if she'd paid more attention to Fenn when she'd first come to take me, that would be different. But she'd barely even given him a glance.

"Good idea," Rosemary said. "Do you know where he is right now?"

I shook my head. "But maybe Fenn knows?" I didn't want to over rely on the kitsune every time I had a problem, but so far he'd known what I needed and when. It was worth a try. "Do you, boy?" I asked.

His tails moved from side to side quickly.

"Is that a yes or a no?" Eliza mused.

I shrugged. "Your guess is as good as mine, I'm still trying to work out what he means half of the time. No one thought to provide me with an instruction manual." Hopefully, once I was living at the palace full time, I'd be able to get some help from the people who worked in the stables. That was where he'd lived before deciding to imprint on me.

"That's a shame. At least he makes up for it in cuteness," Rosemary quipped.

"Let me get my shoes on," Eliza said.

I waited by the door, with Fenn skipping around my feet, raring to go. I hoped that meant he *did* know where Archie was, not that he simply wanted to play.

I slipped my hand into my pocket and closed my fingers around the small bottle of silver blood. It was still there. I hadn't been imagining the whole thing while the powder Mother used on me wore off.

"Ready," Eliza said.

A small part of me was terrified of the idea that Mother might be waiting behind the door, or around the corner. But that was ridiculous. And exactly why I'd asked Fenn to take me to Rosemary instead of back to my own room. It felt safer to be with other people.

I took a deep breath and opened the door, ready to follow Fenn to wherever Archie was.

CHAPTER EIGHTEEN

Fenn didn't stop until we were outside the door to what seemed like it was a private office. I held up my hand to stop the other two from making a sound. I could hear voices, and I wanted to know what they were saying before barging in and making myself known.

"This has gone on long enough. You're to make your decision tonight," the King said.

"It's been less than a week, Father," Archie countered.

"True. And yet we have two commoners and a nobody in the top five."

"Because I've known this entire time who I was going to pick," he countered.

"Oh good. That Felicia girl, I assume. You were close as children."

"No." I imagined Archie clenching his jaw as he spoke. "Lady Cosette."

"I wouldn't bother," Felicia said, sounding like she was entering the room from another direction. "She's gone."

"Gone?" Archie echoed. "I doubt that."

"I was just in her room, and found a note..."

I exchanged a confused look with Eliza. "Was there one when you were there?" I whispered.

She shook her head. "Not that I saw, but I didn't look around a lot." Guilt washed over her face. "Do you know how to write?"

There was no point letting her question get to me. It was a valid one, and I knew it was coming from a practical place and not a judgmental one. She really did want to know if there was a possibility I hadn't written it. That would be the easiest solution.

"I can, yes."

"Ah."

"I guess it's time to go in," I said to the two of them. "Are you sure you want to do this? I don't want either of you missing out on anything because of me." I looked between them, hoping they'd back me, but not blaming them if they didn't. I'd think twice about it in their shoes.

Maybe.

"We're with you all the way," Eliza promised. "We

both have more to gain from standing by your side, than to lose by standing against her."

"Thank you." I reached out and squeezed each of their hands in turn. "Please don't do this because of what I know."

"We're not," Rosemary promised.

With their assurances, I reached out and rapped on the door. It only took a moment for the footman to pull it open.

"What can I do for you, My Ladies?" he asked.

"We'd like an audience with the King and the Prince, if that's possible," I said as politely as I could, making sure my voice was loud enough for Archie to hear, even from this distance. The last thing I wanted was to be turned away without him knowing I was here.

Fenn seemed to have reached the same decision, as he darted into the room and headed in the direction I assumed Archie was standing in.

"I shall see if they're willing to receive you." He turned away and followed in the same direction as Fenn had just gone. After a murmured conversation, he returned. "They'll see you now."

"Thank you." I dipped my head in acknowledgement.

A small smile lifted the corners of his lips. I was

glad I could brighten his day with something so simple.

The three of us followed him into the room. I placed each foot in front of the other carefully, trying to look as elegant as possible despite the state of my gown. Perhaps I should have returned to my own room after all, then I could have gotten a new gown and looked the part.

But no. I'd have given up a chance to show everyone what Felicia was up to if I'd done that.

The King sat in a high backed chair in front of the fireplace, while Felicia stood next to him, and Archie crouched down fussing Fenn.

"Lady Cosette, I was just informed you were no longer in the palace," the King said.

The moment Archie's gaze locked on me, his whole face lit up. I was only half watching him, though. The rest of my attention was on his Father and the raised eyebrow he was giving his son. It appeared I wasn't the only one who had noticed Archie's reaction to me.

"Unfortunately, I was briefly detained away from the castle, but it was through no desire of my own. I believe that someone conspired with my Mother to kidnap me and return me to the tower I'd been kept in my entire life." There was no point dressing up what I was saying when there would be a direct accusation soon after.

"Why would anyone wish to kidnap you, Lady Cosette?" Felicia asked sweetly. But I didn't miss the flash of menace in her eyes. She didn't like that I was here. Nor that I clearly knew her secret.

"For this. I imagine." I pulled the bottle of silver blood from my pocket and set it on the small table next to the King. "At least, that is what I believe Mother's motive is. As far as I can tell, she's been harvesting blood from me while I've been asleep for years, then selling it. All without my knowledge."

Archie sucked in a breath. "That's illegal."

Oh. I hadn't realised that.

"I only found out about it today," I promised.

The King gestured for his man-servant. "Please send a team of guards to Lady Cosette's home residence and investigate. If there is any evidence of silver blood selling, then they're to arrest anyone they find there and bring them here for questioning."

The man-servant dipped his head. "Where is Lady Cosette's residence?" he asked.

Everyone turned to look at me, and my cheeks burned. I still didn't know where the village was.

"I..." My gaze met Archie's. Other than Fenn, he was the only person who had any chance of knowing the answer to that question.

"Rivertown," Archie put in. "A tower about a mile south of there."

"I'll see that it's done," the man-servant said, then vanished out into the hall.

"Thank you," I mouthed at Archie.

He smiled in return, reassuring me that someone was on my side.

"Who do you believe the other person was in this kidnap plot?" the King prompted.

"One of the ladies taking part in the competition," I admitted, unsure if I really wanted to name Felicia when she was in the room.

"Why would any of the ladies here conspire with your Mother to take you from your room?" Felicia asked, a delicate eyebrow raised.

"She never said she was taken from her room," Archie said softly.

"Indeed." The King turned his attention to the other woman.

Her normally calm demeanour became flustered as her error sunk in. She was going to have to think fast if she wanted to get out of this one quickly.

"I have a witness who overheard the two conspiring," I offered.

Eliza stepped forward and the King sighed.

"Is this true, Lady Felicia?" he asked.

She stared at the ground, scuffing her foot against the floor. "Yes."

"Why?" Archie sounded pained, and I longed to go over to him and soothe it away.

The confusion and frustration in Felicia's eyes as she looked longingly at Archie lanced through my heart. She couldn't be having a good time of it. Especially not with all the attention on her.

"I wanted you to notice me," she said.

I was torn between anger and pity, and had no idea which would win out.

The King sighed loudly again. "Isn't this a mess."

It was a statement and not a question, so we all stayed silent. Even Fenn didn't move as he stood next to me.

"Archibald, you can make your choice without my influence. Lady Felicia, I'm sorry, but you are disqualified from the competition. Because of your parents' positions at court, you won't be punished further, but you will have to seek permission from the sovereign should you choose to wed," he said.

"Thank you, Your Majesty," she said contritely.

"Now, if that is all, I have other things which need attending to." He got to his feet, and swept out of the room, leaving us all behind without another word.

Archie deflated, and I took the chance to go over

to him. He wrapped his arms tightly around me, and I returned the gesture. Fenn even pressed himself against our legs to join in the embrace.

I lost track of how long we stood there, but I was dimly aware of the others leaving.

But it no longer mattered. The game had been played, and I had won. Now I'd be spending the rest of my life with Archie. Just like we both wanted.

CHAPTER NINETEEN

ARCHIE KNOCKED on the open door to my new rooms. "Can I come in?"

"Of course. I do believe the *point* is that you can come and go when you please," I pointed out.

"That doesn't change anything if it isn't what *you* want, though."

"I appreciate the thought." I smiled at him, and then flopped down on the comfortable sofa next to Fenn.

He looked up at the new intruder, but then dismissed him as someone of interest and went back to sleep. I scratched the top of his head absent-mindedly.

"I'm guessing you've not got good news."

He grimaced, then sat down next to me. "No."

I sighed. That should be expected. I knew what

Mother was like at the best of times, and now her freedom was on the line, it'd be even worse.

"What did she say?" I needed to hear it fast, or I'd chicken out and not want him to mention it at all.

"The same as she's been saying since she got here. She isn't denying that she's been selling your blood. There's too much evidence for that not to be true. Plus, we have at least three witnesses now who heard her talking about it."

I sighed. "But she's refusing to say anything about the kidnapping. Or why she didn't just tell me what she's doing."

"I asked if she wanted to talk to you," he admitted. "I thought it might open her up a bit."

"Let's guess....that didn't work either?" A note of bitterness swept into my voice.

Archie put an arm around me and pulled me close before dropping a kiss against my temple. "No. She refuses to talk to you."

A lone tear rolled down my cheek and splashed onto the fabric of my dress.

Fenn sensed my mood and shifted so he could lay his head over my lap. I closed my eyes and accepted the affection from my kitsune on one side, and my fiancé on the other. At least I had the two of them to rely on, even if my own Mother was ready to disown me.

I wiped away the other tears which threatened. "I'm sorry, I was expecting it, but it still hurts."

"I would have thought she'd be more accommodating now that her daughter is a future queen." He paused, as if wondering whether or not he should say something. "We can let her go, if you want," he said softly.

"No." The word came out stronger than I expected, startling poor Fenn.

I scratched behind his ears, and he settled back down again.

"I don't trust her," I admitted. "If we let her go, then I'd always be looking over my shoulder, wondering what she was up to next, and if she'd try to take me away from you again. There are plenty of people at court who would team up with her now you've made your choice. I doubt Rebekah is too happy."

"Definitely not. She's run away from court and is sulking, I believe."

A sad smile spread over my face. "She could have been so much more than she made herself into."

"So could Felicia," he pointed out. "I should have seen the warning signs."

"Maybe. But you can't blame yourself for that really," I countered. "You still saw her as the girl you helped."

"Perhaps."

I turned my head and pressed a kiss against his cheek. "She'll forgive us in time."

"Surely it's you who should be forgiving her?" he muttered.

"I already have." Being part of the competition hadn't been good for Felicia. It might not have been for others if they'd stayed longer either.

"Then you're a better person than I am," he admitted.

"That's not true at all."

He sighed, but didn't say anything more. I knew this was going to plague us for a while, but I knew we'd work through it in the end. It wasn't our faults that Felicia hadn't liked the way things had gone. Or that she'd chosen to team up with my Mother to kidnap me. But at the end of the day, we were the ones who needed to take the high road, and that's what I was determined to do.

"Are you ready for tomorrow?" he asked suddenly.

"The ball to officially welcome me as your fiancée?" I checked, as if it could be anything else.

"Yes. This is your last chance to decide to run away."

I chuckled. "That isn't something I plan on doing," I assured him. "I'm looking forward to it.

Eliza and Rosemary are both coming back today with their things so they can move into the Lady-in-waiting's chambers." I didn't mention to him that it would give them a good excuse to spend a lot of alone time together. That was still their secret to keep.

"I'm glad they'll be here to keep you company," he said.

"But for now, I have to put up with you," I teased.

He chuckled deeply, the sound vibrating through him.

I leaned in and pressed my lips against his. My eyes fluttered closed as we relaxed into one another. His hand trailed over my cheek, until he tangled one of his hands in my hair, using it to pull me closer and deepen our kiss. It was different from the kisses we'd shared in the village, or even the one in the lake here. It was almost like we'd realised we could take our time here. No one was going to stop us from showing our affection to one another.

"I love you, Cosette," he whispered against my lips.

"I love you too," I responded, then resumed our kiss.

EPILOGUE

"Introducing His Royal Highness, Prince Archibald, and his fiancée, Lady Cosette," the herald called.

"Ready?" Archie whispered to me.

"As I'll ever be," I promised. "You know, it's still weird to hear you being called Archibald all the time."

He chuckled. "I promise, you'll get used to it."

"And the weight of all these jewels?" I asked. The Queen and his sister had insisted on decking me out in one of the sets of crown jewels, even though I wasn't technically allowed to wear a tiara yet. They seemed to have learned I didn't have any jewellery of my own, and decided to change that.

The only problem was that it weighed a tonne. If I moved my ears too quickly, I'd probably end up tearing them open with the size of the gems dangling from them.

"I can't say I know much about that," he admitted as he swept me into the room. "I can promise you they look divine on you, though."

I smiled at that. I did look good. The green ball gown fit me perfectly, despite the short amount of time the seamstresses had to make it. And I shimmered in the candlelight. Partly due to the jewels, but also because of the fabric they'd used. When I'd looked in the mirror before leaving my rooms, I had thought I was looking at a future royal, not a pauper who had been trapped in a tower and happened to have found herself at court.

"Are you ready to dance?" he asked.

"So long as you don't expect me to be any better than last week," I joked.

He chuckled lightly. "Was it only a week?"

"Yes. But I hope you know that means I'm going to expect you to teach me how to dance properly before the next one of these. I don't want to embarrass you."

"You won't." He pulled me into his arms and we began to sway along with the music. "You could never embarrass me," he murmured so only I could hear.

People joined us in the dance, allowing me to

relax a little. It was easier not to have all the eyes on me, even if I knew that was unlikely at a ball which was celebrating my engagement to Archie.

I glanced over his shoulder in time to see Eliza pulling Rosemary into a dance. A smile stretched over my face at the sight of them. They were truly happy, and I was glad I got to see it.

Archie stopped the dance, despite the fact we were in the middle of the other couples. He gazed down at me with so much love and devotion in his eyes, it would be impossible for me *not* to realise how good our future would be.

He leaned down and pressed his lips against mine. I lost myself in him, only dimly aware of the music and the surrounding couples. They hardly even registered in my thoughts.

We didn't break away from one another until something pressed against our lower legs.

I opened my eyes to find Fenn darting around with a mischievous look on his face.

"You were supposed to stay in the room," I told him.

"Like he's ever going to listen." Amusement shone through Archie's voice. "And to think, I have to put up with this for the rest of my life.

"Just wait until we have children." I leaned up and pressed a kiss against his cheek.

The ever after might only just be beginning, but I could already tell it was going to be a good one. And I planned on making the most of it.

* * *

The End

* * *

Thank you for taking the time to read *Braided Silver*, I hope you enjoyed it! The next book in the *Untold Tales* series is *Fractured Core*, a retelling of Snow White: http://books2read.com/fracturedcore

AUTHOR NOTE

Thank you so much for reading *Braided Silver*, I hope you enjoyed it! This book was so much fun for me to write, especially as it brought together so many of my favourite things - Rapunzel (my favourite fairy tale!), fluffy pets, and Princess competitions! I've always wanted to write the latter, and now I've finally had a chance. If, like me, you love Rapunzel retellings, then I also have another one called *Tower Of Thorns*. It's a fantasy academy romance and book one of my *Once Upon An Academy* series. It's set in a completely different world. and Cosette and Rapunzel (the main characters) are completely different people. But, as a special thank you for taking the time to read the author note, you can download it for free here: https://dl.bookfunnel.com/fducx7tmvv

AUTHOR NOTE

I'd also like to say a big thank you to Jennifer M. who named Fenn after I made a post in my Facebook Reader Group! You can join for other chances at naming characters, as well as release day giveaways and other updates: https://facebook.com/groups/theparanormalcouncil

Braided Silver came about while I was taking part in the *Once Upon A Fairy Tale Night* collection (please note that some books, including *Braided Silver* which was previously titled *Braids Of Silver*, may have been rebranded or retitled now the collection has finished) - each book features a different fairy tale retelling, each with a standalone romance. The books span multiple romance sub-genres, so there's something for everyone, including books from some of my co-authors - Skye MacKinnon (*Song Of Souls*), L.A. Boruff (*Lady Of Outlaws*), and Lacey Carter Andersen (*Spin My Gold*, along with Helen Scott), as well as one from one of my other author besties, Bea Paige (*Cabin Of Axes*). You can check out the rest of the *Once Upon A Fairy Tale Night* books here: http://books2read.com/rl/onceuponafairytalenight

Finally, if you want more fantasy fairy tale retellings like *Braided Silver*, then it isn't my only one! It's actually part of a six book series called *Untold Tales*, which starts with *Balanced Scales* (http://books2read.com/balancedscales), a retelling of The

AUTHOR NOTE

Little Mermaid. Each book in the series follows a different fairy tale, with a standalone happy ever after. And I have lots more fairy tales and fantasy romance to come!

Hope to see you along for the ride again soon!

Thank you for reading,

Laura

ALSO BY LAURA GREENWOOD

Books in the Obscure World

- Ashryn Barker Trilogy (urban fantasy, completed series)
- Grimalkin Academy: Kittens Series (paranormal academy, completed series)
- Grimalkin Academy: Catacombs Trilogy (paranormal academy, completed series)
- City Of Blood Trilogy (urban fantasy)
- Grimalkin Academy: Stakes Trilogy (paranormal academy)
- The Harpy Bounty Hunter Trilogy (urban fantasy)
- The Black Fan (vampire romance)
- Sabre Woods Academy (paranormal academy)
- Scythe Grove Academy (urban fantasy)
- Carnival Of Knives (urban fantasy)

Books in the Forgotten Gods World

- The Queen of Gods Trilogy (paranormal/mythology romance)

- Forgotten Gods Series (paranormal/mythology romance)

The Grimm World

- Grimm Academy Series (fairy tale academy)
- Fate Of The Crown Duology (Arthurian academy, completed series)
- Once Upon An Academy Series (fairy tale academy)

Books in the Paranormal Council Universe

- The Paranormal Council Series (shifter romance)
- The Fae Queen Of Winter Trilogy (paranormal/fantasy, completed series)
- Thornheart Coven Series (witch romance)
- Return Of The Fae Series (paranormal post-apocalyptic, completed series)
- Paranormal Criminal Investigations Series (urban fantasy mystery)
- MatchMater Paranormal Dating App Series (paranormal romance, completed series)
- The Necromancer Council Trilogy (urban

fantasy)
- Standalone Stories From the Paranormal Council Universe

Other Series

- The Apprentice Of Anubis (urban fantasy in an alternate world)
- Beyond The Curse (dark fantasy fairy tale)
- Untold Tales Series (fantasy fairy tales, completed series)
- The Dragon Duels Trilogy (urban fantasy dystopia)
- ME Contemporary Standalones (contemporary romance)
- Standalones
- Seven Wardens, co-written with Skye MacKinnon (paranormal/fantasy romance, completed series)
- Tales Of Clan Robbins, co-written with L.A. Boruff (urban fantasy Western)
- The Firehouse Feline, co-written with Lacey Carter Andersen & L.A. Boruff (paranormal/urban fantasy romance, completed series)
- Kingdom Of Fairytales Snow White, co-

written with J.A. Armitage (fantasy fairy tale, completed series)

Twin Souls Universe

- Twin Souls Trilogy, co-written with Arizona Tape (paranormal romance, completed series)
- Dragon Soul Series, co-written with Arizona Tape (paranormal romance, completed series)
- The Renegade Dragons Trilogy, co-written with Arizona Tape (paranormal romance, completed series)
- The Vampire Detective Trilogy, co-written with Arizona Tape (urban fantasy mystery, completed series)
- Amethyst's Wand Shop Mysteries Series, co-written with Arizona Tape (urban fantasy)

Mountain Shifters Universe

- Valentine Pride Trilogy, co-written with L.A. Boruff (paranormal shifter romance, completed series)
- Magic and Metaphysics Academy Trilogy,

co-written with L.A. Boruff (paranormal academy, completed series)
- Mountain Shifters Standalones, co-written with L.A. Boruff (paranormal romance)

Audiobooks: www.authorlauragreenwood.co.uk/p/audio.html

ABOUT THE AUTHOR

Laura is a USA Today Bestselling Author of paranormal, fantasy, and urban fantasy romance (though she can occasionally be found writing contemporary romance). When she's not writing, she drinks a lot of tea, tries to resist French macarons, and works towards a diploma in Egyptology. She lives in the UK, where most of her books are set.

FOLLOW THE AUTHOR

- Website: www.authorlauragreenwood.co.uk
- Mailing List: www.authorlauragreenwood.co.uk/p/mailing-list-sign-up.html
- Facebook Group: http://facebook.com/groups/theparanormalcouncil
- Facebook Page: http://facebook.com/authorlauragreenwood

- Bookbub: www.bookbub.com/authors/laura-greenwood
- Instagram: www.instagram.com/authorlauragreenwood
- Twitter: www.twitter.com/lauramg_tdir

Printed in Great Britain
by Amazon